LIGHTHOUSE

MYSTERY

Harald Lutz Bruckner

Lighthouse Mystery

Published by Hideaway Park Press
Green Valley, AZ

ISBN: 978-1-0878-6332-0 (paperback)
ISBN: 978-1-0878-6333-7 (ebook)
LCCN: 2020902115

Books by Harald Lutz Bruckner

The Blue Sapphire Amulet

The Birken Saga
A Trilogy

Book 1 *Escape on the Astral Express*
Book 2 *A Wanderer on the Earth*
Book 3 *The Born-Again Phoenix*

Harald's Garland

Lighthouse Mystery

To Nina, Steven, Gerry, and Mark

Chapter 1

HOMER Annapolis emerged from the lighthouse, tightly holding the hand of his beloved wife, Sylvia. She glanced at him sideways. "You must have gotten dressed in a hurry. Look at you. The brass buttons on your uniform jacket are off by one. Here, let me straighten them out and help you make yourself presentable, not that anyone will be calling on us. Oh, my goodness. That cap of yours covers a multitude of sins as well. I believe you are dearly in need of a haircut!"

He smiled at her, inwardly liking being fussed over by his wife of many years. "I couldn't wait to get out and see what Mother Nature visited upon us during the last few days. That was quite the storm that blew in from the west. I wonder if any ships were out there that couldn't make out the powerful beam from the new lighthouse below us? I'm so glad the heavy fog is finally lifting. Can you see the rugged coastline way down there? I wish I had my glasses."

"Yes, I can. The surf is still pounding mightily against those ancient rocks. Let me fetch your glasses; then you can see for yourself. You must've been really in a hurry not to have slipped them on when you rose from your sleep sack."

Homer stood still for a moment, staring into the distance as Sylvia disappeared into the old lighthouse. He looked at his wrinkled uniform pants and mumbled, "I better use my slickers before I hike down to the shore and take in the damage left by last night's storm."

Sylvia rushed to his side and gently placed his pince-nez on his masculine nose. "There, dear man, that ought to be better. What did you decide to do while I went inside?"

"I'm heading down to the shore to take a look-see. No need for you to mess up your boots and dress. It looks like you just washed and pressed this lovely frock. I'll slip on some oilskins over my pants, although they look like they could stand a wash and a loving press from the hefty iron you keep on hand." He didn't wait for Sylvia's response.

He turned away from her, heading for the shed to retrieve his waterproof skins. Minutes later, Sylvia waved at Homer as he began his descent toward the sea. The wind blew his cap smack off his head, exposing a shock of snow-white hair. Picking up his mariner cap from the damp ground, Homer slapped his treasured head covering back into place. Sylvia couldn't help laughing as she took in the whole scene.

Losing his cap was bad enough; he was thankful Sylvia couldn't see him sliding onto his hind end as the saturated and slippery ground gave way under his boots. *"Damn it,"* escaped his lips. He wasn't inclined to cuss, and certainly not in the presence of his dear Sylvia. He scrambled back on his feet and continued his trek toward the shoreline. Obviously, it was high tide and giant whitecaps still forced their might against the unforgiving cliffs and ate mercilessly into the white sands of the beach.

Homer thought he wasn't seeing right. He adjusted the seat of his glasses, but nothing changed. A few hundred feet from his vantage point he spotted a good-sized cutter swept onto the strand not too distant from the craggy rocks that would have spelled total destruction. *I didn't hear any distress signals or a foghorn before we retired,* Homer pondered as he tried to pick up his pace against the howling wind.

He was breathing hard as he reached the stranded vessel and began to vocalize, trying to get the attention of anyone manning the boat. Its two masts had been toppled by the power of the storm that wreaked total destruction on top deck. "Ahoy! Ahoy! Anyone there?" Homer kept yelling again and again. But all he could hear was the sound of crashing waves as they rushed ashore.

Homer wasn't sure if he could tackle climbing aboard the vessel, especially being alone. Against his better judgment, he searched for large-enough debris washed onto the beach, allowing him to create a ramp and easier access to the deck of the stranded boat.

Having overcome the initial challenge, he carefully picked his way through all the trash covering the deck. One of his feet got caught in a pile of seaweed. He was very much aware of the kelp forest near the shore. He held onto the steering wheel as he took a gander into the open door to the relatively shallow hull. Homer pushed aside a large piece of wood apparently splintered off one of the broken masts and stepped down, slowly entering the space below and casting a look around. Broken glasses and cups were scattered on the floor. There was no evidence of any human habitation.

He kicked aside some of the larger shards, as he aimed toward the bulkhead and a closed curtain on its left side.

Homer needed to know what lay beyond the heavy draped fabric dividing the hull into two chambers. As he pushed the rings suspending the weighty material to his right, he could dimly make out a body lying on the floor of the cutter. *Darn, why didn't I grab my flashlight?* He admonished himself as he carefully backed away from the scene, not wanting to touch another thing with his ungloved hands.

Homer prepared himself for the challenging hike uphill, and he knew what he needed to do. Undoubtedly, this was a case for the local police, and perhaps even forces beyond the present scene. Sylvia marveled and smiled as she watched her octogenarian lover climb up the hill from the shores of Cabrillo National Monument.

She decided to wait for him inside the lighthouse rather than see him tumble and slip on the slippery ground one more time. Sylvia was fully aware of his short temper when things no longer went the way they did when he was a much younger man. She often told him to take a good look in the mirror. He didn't like to be reminded of the fact that many years had indeed gone by.

Sylvia looked upon Homer with pride. *I've spent a lifetime with you, dear man. I cannot believe the things you continue to tackle at your age.* At that moment, her mind took her back sixty-one years.

"I met Homer in San Francisco in 1907. His parents' home on Sanchez Street had survived the earthquake. He had been lighthouse keeper at Point Arena for only two years, when the 1906 earthquake destroyed his cherished place of work.

Homer Elias was the only single man on duty. Two of the other lighthouse keepers were married and had young kids. A third couple had three adult children. Two sons were living in San Francisco; only a daughter, Jenna, was still living at the lighthouse with her parents. All who lived at the lighthouse barely escaped the collapsing tower when the quake struck.

"Homer Elias was the handsomest man that walked this earth. We fell in love at first sight and were married within weeks. I can still hear him tell me what his greatest hopes and desires were. 'Sylvia, you may not be delighted to hear this, but I've always wanted to be a lighthouse keeper. When Point Arena went down, I knew in my heart that I would return someday.'

"And so, it came to pass that the lighthouse was rebuilt to much safer standards and reopened in 1908. Homer was overjoyed to carry me as his wife across the threshold of the resurrected lighthouse. During the daytime, Homer would be busy working with the other men, but at night he was all mine.

"I had always hoped to have children of my own, a pleasure the gods unfortunately denied us. The wheel became my trusted friend, as I spent many hours spinning the wool gathered from the sheep that grazed not too far from Point Arena. Homer eventually bought me a weaving loom. How I enjoyed creating things for the children of the families who lived with us at the lighthouse. I was particularly fond of a little boy who could have been Homer's; the resemblance was uncanny.

"Joshua was born to Jenna, daughter of the oldest of the lighthouse keepers, in 1905. The boy came to his good looks from his mother, a striking blonde who was of Swedish descent. I can still see her with her thick braids, Joshua always wanting to play with his mother's tresses when she held him close to her generous breasts. What I didn't realize at first was that Joshua's mother encouraged him to spend much time with us, especially when Homer was around.

"Sometimes Joshua would climb on Homer's lap, thrilled to be held by a man, thrilled to be fed by Homer. I would look at the two in profile, only to realize one day that Joshua had sprung from my husband's loins. I began asking the other women as to the whereabouts of Joshua's father and received nothing but vague answers. Joshua, Jenna, and the unknown father were taboo subjects no one wanted to touch.

"By the time Joshua was of school age, there was no longer any question who had blessed the boy with his handsome visage; he bore the striking hair color of his Swedish mother and his marked facial structures were those of his father.

"One may have thought I would be plagued with jealousy, but I wasn't, since Homer and I were blissfully happy in our daily togetherness. I knew that he loved me from the moment we first met. As the years went by, I realized that I would never bear Homer any children, and deep in my heart I was thankful that he had fathered a beautiful and healthy boy long before I ever came into the picture. While Jenna and I never became close friends, we treated each other with respect and civility. Once I was absolutely certain that she and Homer were Joshua's creators, I never raised any questions with either of them.

"When Homer was drafted into the Great War in 1915, he confronted me. 'I've known for many years that you discovered that Joshua is my son. Jenna and I had a single night of pleasure when I was just twenty-one years old. It was during my first year at Point Arena. I didn't know that I had fathered the boy since Jenna saw several young men at the time. When we fled Point Arena after the quake, the child was barely one year old. Yes, I saw the baby, but never knew that I was his father. It was only after you and I were married and returned to the lighthouse that I could see a certain resemblance in the three-year-old boy. I'm certain, even Jenna wasn't sure who Joshua's father was until he became a toddler and his features unquestionably resembled mine. Her parents never challenged me, being fully aware of Jenna's lust for men. Joshua is their only grandchild at this time. His grandfather told me a few years ago that he was glad to know the bloke who fathered his grandson.'

"We were lucky; Homer was considered over the hill at age thirty-two. Between his age and showing with flat feet, he was excused from having to serve in the army. He was advised that his expertise could be applied much more productively by continuing to man the Point Arena Lighthouse.

"The next three years were among the happiest in our marriage. Homer and I were in the prime of our lives and thoroughly enjoyed every opportunity of celebrating married bliss. Joshua was going on eleven when he confronted his father. 'When I look in the mirror, I see you. Are you the father I've never been told about? If you are my father, I want you to know that I've loved you from the moment I was old enough to climb onto your lap.' Homer hugged him and kissed his forehead and held the boy as tightly as he could. Joshua knew he was home at last.

"Tragedy struck our idyllic and harmonious life at the lighthouse when the Spanish influenza struck in 1918. I must have been singled out not to be touched by the devastating illness; I became Florence Nightingale of the lighthouse. Instead of sitting at the spinning wheel or weaving on my loom, I was nursing the ill. Four of the adults and five of the children on site I couldn't save, in spite of all I tried to keep them alive. Joshua lost his mother and his maternal grandparents. One of the uncles in San Francisco was taken as well.

"Homer and I talked with Joshua, now a young man going on thirteen, about his willingness to become part of our family. We legally adopted Joshua in 1920. He filled a spot in my heart that had laid barren for all those years. He was baptized and confirmed in the Lutheran faith at age fifteen. Joshua was a bright young man and excelled in school. While he loved the sea as much as his father, he didn't want to become a lighthouse keeper. Living up to his name, he became a cadet at Annapolis and we were among the proudest parents when Joshua graduated as an ensign and a commissioned officer in the US Navy in 1928. He was married to dear Loretta two years later. We became grandparents when Samuel Luke was born in 1934. Our granddaughter Mary Henrietta came into our lives two years later.

"Joshua was a lieutenant commander on the USS *Arizona* when she was struck on December 7, 1941. It was a day I shall never forget, a day that changed all our lives forever. Loretta never remarried but dedicated her life to making her children responsible citizens. Samuel followed in his father's footsteps and sails the seven seas these days, being a captain on an atomic submarine. It scares the heck out of Homer and me, but we know, he's doing what he wants to do. It's in his blood. Mary Henrietta has given us two beautiful great-grandchildren. Our lives are fulfilled. Both, well into our eighties, it seems we are still married to the sea."

Chapter 2

CATCHING his breath, Homer faced Sylvia, sitting at her spinning wheel. Her mind was still reliving the twists and turns in their own past lives. "You look like a ghost," she said as she looked at her usually unshakable husband. "What happened down by the beach? What did you encounter?" Her brow was furrowed as she posed her questions.

Homer told her about the stranded cutter and what he discovered once he had gotten onto the boat. "What I saw is obviously outside my jurisdiction. I'm on my way to town. You stay here. There's nothing you and I can do at this point except to report what I found."

Sylvia was imagining the scene Homer had encountered on the stranded boat. *A scuttled vessel bearing the body of another human. Who could this person be? What might have happened?* She couldn't wait to learn more.

Homer retrieved one of their bikes from the shed and easily hopped on the seat. *This is much better than hiking down and up that steep hill between the lighthouse and the shore. I wonder why*

Sylvia looked so saddened and worried when I shared with her what I discovered. Ten minutes later, he rested his trusted bike against the building housing the local police department and headed straight for the office of the commander, whom he knew well. He knocked on the heavy-oaken door—and not too gently. "Enter," was the singular response. There was no "please."

Homer did as told and looked at Howard Shepherd seated behind a large and very disorderly desk heaped with hundreds of papers. Howard's reputation for being a regular slob was often the talk of the village, although he was widely respected by his staff, his superiors, and the people whom he served.

"What brings you into town, Homer? Don't you have better and more important things to keep you busy after that horrendous storm? Did you suffer any damage at the old lighthouse? It isn't Sylvia, or is it?"

"Sylvia is doing just fine, and the lighthouse is still standing proudly. I hiked down to the shore and located a heavily damaged craft stranded on the beach not too far from the cliffs. After a challenging climb onto the darn thing, I discovered a body lying on the floor of the hull; that is, it's in a chamber beyond the bulkhead. The light was rather dim, and I didn't carry a torch. I couldn't even make out if it was man or woman. All I can tell you is that there is a body lying in the bottom of that boat.

"I never touched a thing with my bare hands inside the chamber except the wooden rings suspending the heavy drape that separates the 'death chamber'—so to speak—from the rest of the hull. I rest my case, Howard. It's in your hands." Saying that, Homer rubbed and flipped the palms of his hands downward, underscoring his last statement.

"I get it, Homer. My men and I are on it. I appreciate your reporting posthaste what you discovered. We'll follow you in the paddy wagon. Just give me a minute to set my men in motion."

Chapter 3

Sylvia heard the slam of the shed door, Homer having put his bicycle back into place. And then she became aware of the humming noise made by the engine of the paddy wagon. She decided to step away from her spinning wheel to see what was happening outside. Commander Shepherd jumped from the vehicle and briefly, but courteously, greeted her. "Morning, Ma'am. Interesting news Homer delivered. Not to worry; my men and I will take care of things."

"Thanks, Commander. We knew you would get to the bottom of this." She didn't say more since Shepherd had already stepped away from her, leading three of his policemen down the hill toward the stranded cutter. Homer looked at her: "Interesting news for sure. I'm ready for my second cup of coffee. That wind is still chilling to the bone." *Interesting indeed; I'm dying to learn what Shepherd and his men will unearth.*

⋊⋉

As soon as the men of the law reached the shore, Shepherd

took charge. "Set down the stretcher and let's see if we can strengthen that temporary ramp Homer created. Perhaps it was sturdy enough for him but surely not for you or me, Harry. Both of us are a bit too hefty for that contraption that our good guide of the old lighthouse used. I'm not willing to have us break any joints in the process of this investigation."

Tony, the youngest of the policemen, offered to charge up the hill and retrieve two planks they had brought from the station. Shepherd was pleased with himself to have had foresight. Now he was stomping around the stranded vessel, anxiously waiting to lay eyes on the mysterious corpse. He spotted the twelve-digit hull identification number, (HIN) #879 47654 0449, somewhat faded with time and scribbled it down as the first entry on the clipboard he had clutched under his left arm. At last, Tony arrived, heavily breathing under the weight of the two planks he had carried down the steep hill. "How come those planks are so muddy?" Shepherd inquired.

"Sorry, boss. I wound up on my ass on that slippery slope— and not just once, but twice! Sorry about the muddy boards."

"Well, let's get them in place and see what we can find."

Tony and Harry made sure the planks were firmly placed against the side of the boat and tested soundness of the ramp by using it themselves to get on deck. "It's OK boss. Come aboard!" Harry made a welcoming gesture by swinging his right arm, inviting Shepherd to step onto the slightly listing sailing craft. The third man, Walter Sconce, stayed off the wreck, making sure nothing had shifted on the primitive ramp his colleagues had conceived.

Shepherd entered the hull, having to bend deeply to avoid hitting his head. "Boy, this is pretty confining. Harry, you better let Tony join me in here. You just stand there and listen to what I have to say and make notes on this clipboard." With that he turned toward Harry and handed him the board. "Here, take my jacket, too. All I'll need is the flashlight. Hold on a sec; I need to get some gloves out of my jacket pocket."

He didn't have to open any "curtain"; Homer left it drawn after he made his shocking discovery. Stepping close to the body, lying on its right side, and having turned on the powerful flashlight, Shepherd could tell he was looking at the face of a young woman. Just to make sure, he touched her neck with his gloved hand. No question about it, the woman was dead. He flashed the light over the space surrounding the body, running the light up and down. He could not see evidence of any sort of violence or aggression. Shepherd noted her right hand clasped in a tight fist, the only thing that appeared to be calling attention to itself.

"Harry, have Walter hand you the stretcher. Tony and I will be able to place her corpse on it and remove her from the hull. Once you have her off the wreck, let's cover the body with the sheet we brought to keep insects away from her until we get the remains to the morgue. I want to take another close look around this area after we remove her.

"Tony, after you and Walter carry the victim up to the paddy wagon, bring down the stakes and the yellow tape. For the time being, no one else should step onto this vessel. While I cannot call it a crime scene at this very moment, I want to be sure that none of the boat is touched by any outsiders. For that reason, I want to make sure that anyone coming upon the site understands the "hands off" markers left by us. Let's get her out of here, Tony. You and Walter are lucky; she probably weighs less than ninety pounds.

"Take her by her arms, Tony, and I'll handle her by her legs and feet. Let's lift her carefully; I want her and her surroundings disturbed as little as possible."

"Chief, there is a pouch hanging down from her waist in the back."

"Let's leave it there for now. We'll have the coroner inspect it closely." He made his statement loud enough for Harry and Walter to get his message. Placing the woman's body on the stretcher, he reiterated his earlier comment: "Gentlemen, just make sure the corpse gets to the morgue—and do not touch anything! Do you understand?"

"Yes, Sir." They clicked their heels underscoring their understanding of the chief. Commander Shepherd hesitatingly treaded down the precarious plank and walked once again around the wrecked cutter. He reread the HIN and noted the barely legible name of the boat. He finally deciphered "Arabella" and made a mental note of it.

When he finally made it back to the top of the hill, he was greeted by Homer. "Was it a male or a female?" was his first question.

Howard Shepherd had to catch his breath before he could answer. "It, it, it was—a young woman. And she was indeed dead. That's all I can tell you right now, Homer." Sylvia gasped and turned away, facing the azure sky. Her face was awash in tears.

"Gosh, I'm glad you made sure she was dead. That's probably something I should have checked. Sorry, I was so shocked to see that body; it completely slipped my mind."

"No reason to apologize. That's why you give tours of the lighthouse and I'm the police chief," he winked at Homer Annapolis. "I've got to join the men; we want to get her into the mortuary as quickly as possible. I'll talk on you later."

Homer and Sylvia held hands as they watched the paddy wagon roll down the hill toward town. Neither could have envisioned in their wildest dreams the outcome of the latest storm off the Pacific that struck their shores in recent days. Homer was fully aware how Commander Shepherd's findings had affected his wife.

"I know why you are sad. Your mind is turning back to the most tragic moments in our long life together, the saddest day undoubtedly being November 9, 1941, when those handsome officers appeared at Point Arena Lighthouse to tell us that our dear boy, Joshua, had been among the eleven hundred and two men having gone down with the USS *Arizona* on that day in infamy." Sylvia nodded in agreement.

"No matter how often we've stood on the bridge of that memorial, we still have not found closure to that very sad chapter in our lives. Deep in my heart, I always felt how you loved that boy; he was as much yours as he was mine," said Homer.

Sylvia hugged Homer with all the strength she had in her fragile body. She could feel the wetness of his beautiful face against her shoulders. "Cry all you need to. I cannot strike from my mind what I just learned. My heart goes out to that young woman's loved ones as they will be told of her death and how you discovered her body on that sailboat down there."

Homer wiped his eyes with the right sleeve of his dirty shirt, not saying a word. In his mind's eye he saw Joshua tossing his cap in the air with all the other cadets the day they graduated at Annapolis. That was his way of remembering his dear boy at one of the most joyful moments in all of their lives. He didn't want to imagine Joshua's rotting body in the depth of the Pacific in that far-off place called Pearl Harbor. Sylvia looked pensive as she sat down and activated the wheel with her right foot. She knew for certain what Homer was thinking about.

Chapter 4

OFFICER Harry handed the basically empty clipboard back to the chief. He had recorded only the few observations made by the commander and noted them below the first entry, which was the HIN number. The last entry was the chief's comment that the boat's name was *Arabella*. No one said a word while riding in the vehicle with the corpse of the unknown, dead young woman in the hold. Officers Tony and Walter retrieved a gurney at the station house allowing them to transfer the corpse into the morgue. The coolness of the morbid place was rewarding to all in attendance. Coroner Fortran spoke first: "Is this the body first discovered by Homer Annapolis, the guy who gives tours at the old lighthouse at Point Loma?"

"Yes, it is. Obviously, I'm particularly interested in seeing what the young woman is clutching in her right hand and the content of the pouch she is wearing on her back. More so, I am anxious to see your detailed pathological postmortem report. Guys, let's leave, and let the man do his job. We'll take it from there. I will contact the California DMV and check on the registration of HIN #879 47654 0449 of the boat named *Arabella*.

The men went to wash up and then turned to the canteen to have lunch. Commander Shepherd grinned as he passed his disorderly desk. As soon as he was seated in his comfortable chair, he dialed the phone operator asking to be connected to the offices of the DMV in Orange County.

The phone rang and rang much to his annoyance. When a man finally answered the call, he had been connected to the wrong department. Anyone watching Shepherd would have realized how angry he had become; he was ready to throw the damn phone against the wall. He would have much preferred to speak to someone face-to-face but was fully aware that wasn't possible.

It was a woman who answered: "Esther Smith, DMV, vessel registration. How may I help you?"

"This is Commander Shepherd, precinct #18 in San Diego calling. A cutter with HIN #879 47654 0449 was washed ashore in our area after a terribly destructive storm, apparently abandoned at sea. We are not exactly certain who might have operated or owned the boat. It could have been torn away at its mooring place. We would like to learn in whose name and where the boat was registered."

"Sir, it may take me a while to ascertain this information. Please, let me have your phone number and extension. I will call you back as soon as possible."

"Our number is Trinity 687-4500 and my extension is number one. Thank you. I look forward to hearing from you." Shepherd hung up the phone promptly. Two hours later, Ms. Smith was on the line.

"Commander Shepherd, this is what I was able to find. The cutter named *Arabella* with the HIN number you provided me, is registered to a Mr. Horatio Alvis III who resides in San Luis Obispo. The boat was kept at the Morro Bay Yacht Club. Is this the information for which you were looking?"

"Yes, Ms. Smith. Thank you. You have been very helpful. We'll take it from here. Have a good day."

"Thank you. You too!" and the connection was broken.

The name Horatio Alvis III immediately rang a bell in Shepherd's head. *Wasn't that the name of the guy who ran for the US Senate not too long ago?*

Chapter 5

BY three o'clock, Coroner Fortran and his team had concluded the autopsy and summoned Commander Shepherd to his offices. "Very puzzling case. The pouch you mentioned contained the woman's driver's license, a hundred dollars in various bills and some change, a couple of keys, a lipstick, and a typed note. It reads: 'The enclosed should take care of our little problem.' It was unsigned. On the back of the note, the following was typed as well: George H. Harm, MD. Fertility Consultant (818) 747-4900. She wasn't wearing any rings, but a stunning eighteen-karat gold charm bracelet was on her left wrist. One of the charms, a heart shape, bore the inscription 'With Love – HA III.'

"What she clasped in her right hand was an empty vial. Upon testing it for residue, we discovered it contained cyanide at one time. The use of cyanide by the person in question was confirmed by the presence of the poison on her lips and nostrils. Toxicological testing of her liver provided further evidence that the victim ingested the poison. Based on our examinations of body temperature, rigor mortis, livor mortis (lividity), degree of putrefaction, stomach contents, and corneal cloudiness, we estimate that death occurred twenty-four to thirty-six hours ago. According to the driver's license the young woman carried, she was born on October 23, 1934; that's pretty close to her birthday. She was not quite five months pregnant. Her name was Juliana A. D. Knecht."

Commander Shepherd was speechless. *Cyanide, keys, pregnant, a note, fertility consultant!* "I saw none of this coming. We need to go back to that boat and make sure we didn't overlook any evidence of another's presence. Who knows, someone may have forced her hand in taking the poison."

"We examined her body carefully. There was absolutely no evidence that Juliana was physically harmed or had defended herself against any kind of attacker. We paid particular attention to her fingernails, her torso, and her breasts; there were no signs she had been sexually assaulted. None whatsoever! Examining the fetus, it was a male. Nevertheless, a close search for further supporting evidence possibly present on the boat itself where she apparently died is advisable. Do you have any questions, Howard?"

"Not at the moment, Archibald. If I do, I know where to find you. I have to agree with you, a very puzzling case."

Dr. Fortran covered Juliana's nakedness with a clean sheet and pushed the gurney into the freezing compartment. "By the way, we took some close-up photographs of Ms. Knecht's face. They could come in handy in your investigation. The photo on her driver's license was not the best. The photographer made some copies using an excellent micro-lens; nevertheless, the images are not as sharp as you would want them to be."

"Thanks. I know I can rely on your thoroughness!" *Puzzling, puzzling—indeed!* mumbled Shepherd walking toward his office. He passed Tony Beardsley and knocked firmly on the top of the young officer's desk.

"Got your bike with you? We need to get back to that damn boat. Don't want to miss anything. Let's be sure to take some powerful magnifying glasses and whatever else we may need to take another look at the inside of that vessel."

"Yes, Sir. Will do. With my bike I will find an easier and less taxing way of getting close to the site. I'll be ready to go in ten minutes or so. I'll take the satchel with all the investigative tools we keep in the department. I've got a pouch on the bike that will hold it. Just give me a chance to take a leak before we take off."

"Not a bad idea," said Shepherd, joining Beardsley on his way to the men's room. He filled Tony in on some of the coroner's findings while they were standing at the urinals. So far he had not imparted any of the information in reference to the owner of the sailing craft.

Fifteen minutes later, they arrived at the shore and noted that no one had apparently trespassed the yellow restricting markings. Howard Shepherd was pretty certain that Homer Annapolis kept a close eye on the investigation scene.

A thorough search on deck didn't yield any incriminating evidence; of course, anything that might have been present on deck would have been disbursed by the strong winds or washed away by the sea. There was no evidence of alcoholic consumption, sexual activities, or any kind of physical contact with another person inside the hull. A men's ball cap and a jacket were hanging from a nail on the right side of the space. Tony pocketed a few hairs from these garments and put them into a protective sleeve. They could be matched to possible future suspects in the case. A small, flat box, crumpled gift wrap, and a ribbon had been tossed onto the floor. Maybe the box held a necklace or a similar piece of jewelry at one time.

"Let's pull by the lighthouse. I owe Homer and Sylvia a brief explanation. When we get back to the station, I don't want to be disturbed. I need to digest the information we have so far. I may need to be out of town for a few days. I want you to come with me, and I will put Harry Townsend in charge. He's been next in line for some time; this will give him the opportunity to test the waters of leadership."

"I'll let my girlfriend know regarding our trip. Can you be a bit more specific how long we may be gone? That way I'll know what to pack," said Tony.

"We may be gone two, perhaps three to four days. It all depends on what we discover up north." This was the first hint that Commander Shepherd knew something the others in the precinct were not aware of.

They got on Tony's bike and headed up the hill to the lighthouse. Homer had been standing outside keeping an eye on the activities taking place at the stranded vessel. "Well, Howard, what did you learn? You know more than you did this morning?"

"I'm glad Sylvia keeps busy inside. I'll let you be the judge of what you want to share with her. The young woman, Juliana A. D. Knecht, wasn't quite thirty-four years old. She was in her second trimester of pregnancy and appears to have taken her own life using cyanide. We assume she sailed the craft out of Morro Bay. That's all I can tell you right now. I need to get back to the office and make some contacts. Sorry to be so abrupt but I know you understand. Keep an eye on that wreck down there. Thanks, Homer."

"Howard, I need to be truthful with you. Sylvia and I never

had any secrets in our sixty-one years of marriage—except one. I had a brief affair with a young woman when I was twenty-one. That's a long time ago. It happened three years before I met Sylvia and married her practically on the spot. A boy emerged from that one-night stand and I didn't know about it until the kid was three years old. It was Sylvia who discovered that Joshua was my son; the resemblance to me was uncanny. He had his mother's Swedish blond hair but otherwise he was the spitting image of me. When his mother and her parents fell victim to the Spanish influenza in 1918, Joshua came to us. We adopted him in 1920 and raised him to be a fine young man. We lost him on the USS *Arizona* on December 7, 1941. He was born by the sea and it was the sea that ultimately claimed him. Sylvia and I have already cried over this young woman's body and feel deep in our hearts for her loved ones if and when you will deliver your profound news to them."

Howard put his arms around his sad friend. "I'm so sorry, Homer. I never knew of your tragic story and the death of your son. You and Sylvia always have been very private people. Again, I'm very sorry for your loss. Tony and I have to get back to the office. Give Sylvia a hug from me."

Howard Shepherd hopped on Tony's bike, leaving Homer Annapolis standing next to the old lighthouse, speechless and his shoulders slumped. The commander raised his right hand waving goodbye as Tony pulled away.

Chapter 6

COMMANDER Shepherd motioned his secretary to join him in his office. Alice Walker was his trusted friend in the department. She had seen Howard come up through the ranks. Alice had worked in the police department ever since her husband was killed during the last days of the Korean War in 1953. She and Carl were childless; most of the guys in the department saw her as the mother of them all. While she was very efficient, exceptionally skilled clerically, and always all police business, she had a soft spot in her heart for all the men at precinct #18.

Alice closed the commander's office door quietly and sat across from him, pen and pad in hand. She was ready to spring into action. She couldn't help smirking at Howard's messy desk. *I've given up on that; he's hopeless,* ran through her mind as she smiled at him.

He briefly related to her what he knew so far about the dead woman on the cutter and the apparent origin and connections to the vessel. "First thing you need to research for me is the home address of Horatio Alvis III in San Luis

Obispo. I believe he's one and the same who unsuccessfully ran for the US Senate four years ago. Check for newspaper clippings, anything you can find on this guy. I have no idea what his connection is to this woman, other than the boat that brought her to our shores was registered to a Horatio Alvis III, who kept the sailing vessel named *Arabella* and registered under HIN #879 47654 0449 at the Morro Bay Yacht Club. Get back to me as soon as you know something. I've primed Tony Beardsley to join me on an eventual investigative sojourn up north, and I plan to designate Harry Townsend to be in charge while we are gone. I presume you have no problem with the arrangement?"

"None whatsoever. Harry is a good man and in line for promotional consideration. Acting in your absence might give him the chance. I'll get right on this. I hope to have some answers for you later in the day."

"Oh, there's another matter I'd like you to check. On the back of the typed note was the address of a doctor: George H. Harm, MD. Fertility Consultant (818) 747-4900. Give him a call and see what you can find out." Alice walked to her desk and made her first phone call within minutes.

"San Luis Obispo, Public Library, Erin Drew speaking. How may I direct your call?"

"This is Alice Walker with the San Diego PD Precinct #18. I'm secretary to Commander Shepherd who is investigating a case involving a boat stranded during the most recent storm at our shores. The cutter is registered to a Horatio Alvis III and was apparently moored at the Morro Bay Yacht Club. I am particularly interested in learning the home address of Mr. Alvis. Also, we would like you to search for any press releases and/or references to him that you can access on microfiche and transfer any information to us. We would appreciate your discretion and assistance in this matter."

"Is it Mrs. Walker?"

"Yes, it is."

"I looked up the address for Mr. & Mrs. Horatio Alvis III while I was listening to you. Their address is 18505 Circular Drive in Edmond Valley Estates, San Luis Obispo 93410. The telephone number shown is (805) 617-2043. Please let me know your mailing address, and I'll send you copies of anything I may locate on microfiche."

"Ms. Drew, our mailing address is 2805 History Rd., San Diego, CA 92126. Our telephone number is (619) 945-5200. My extension is number #130. If you have need to reach me, call me collect anytime. We are quite aware of your budgetary limitations. Anything you can find on Mr. Alvis would be of help in the ongoing investigation."

"Thanks, Mrs. Walker. Will do. Good chatting with you. I'll get back with you ASAP. Have a sunny day!"

Alice's next call was to Dr. Harm. The phone rang at least eight times. She almost hung up when a woman finally answered the phone. "Dr. Harm's clinic, how may we help you?"

"My name is Alice Walker; I would like to make an appointment with Dr. Harm."

"I'm sorry, Ma'am, we do not make appointments over the phone. All persons seen by Dr. Harm must arrange for their appointments in person. After consulting with Dr. Harm, he schedules a service date with you. We do not accept any kind of insurance; payment for services must always be in cash. Most consultations run about one thousand dollars." Alice could hear screaming in the background. "You have any other questions, Ma'am? The doctor is calling for my assistance."

"Could you give me the address of your offices?"

"Our clinic is located at 47810 Main Street in South Central LA."

"Thank you for the information." And the connection was gone.

Alice knocked on Commander Shepherd's door in typical fashion. He knew right away who it was wanting to speak to him. "Enter please, Alice! What did you learn so quickly?"

"Nothing real juicy, but I got your man's address and telephone number from the Public Library in San Luis Obispo. A Ms. Drew assisted me and will scroll through their microfiche system. It holds information stored since its inception in 1961; older stuff will be a bit more difficult to access, but she was willing to dig up anything on the Alvis's within her domain. Do you want me to put through a call to the Alvis's or what do you have in mind?"

"Actually, I prefer not to call, but rather appear in person at their doorstep. Getting the address was a real coup. I need a day to digest all that Fortran uncovered and settle an issue that's still bothering me before Beardsley and I leave in an unmarked car Thursday morning. Please ask Tony to see me in my office to discuss details."

"I also contacted the offices of Dr. Harm. I pretended to be in need of services from the good doctor and tried to make an appointment. The conversation with the woman I spoke to was enlightening. Appointments must be made in person, never over the phone. Services are not covered by any insurance, must be paid in cash only, and the average consultation fee runs to be one thousand dollars. Sounds to me like an abortion mill. I got the address where Dr. Harm practices. I would say it's located in one of LA's finest. Does this make any sense to you?"

"It's beginning to. Thank you, Alice."

"You are most welcome, Sir!"

Chapter 7

AFTER another meeting with Coroner Fortran on Wednesday morning, Commander Shepherd was ready to dive into the investigation of the circumstances having led to the death of Juliana A. D. Knecht. "Come in, Tony. I believe we've got all our ducks in order. Alice made short shrift of matters and got us pertinent info re Mr. Alvis III. We'll be leaving at five o'clock tomorrow morning. I want to avoid as much of the LA rush hour traffic as possible. Luck has it, northbound traffic will be lighter. We ought to land sometime in early afternoon in San Luis Obispo. Perhaps we'll arrive at *tea time* or it might be *cocktail hour*. I believe it's a pretty highfalutin neighborhood where the Alvis's reside. So, do your packing tonight. I'll get the car at the station around four-thirty and head straight for your place. Any questions?"

"Nope! Couldn't be any more precise. I'll cut out at four this afternoon. Perhaps Monica and I can have an early dinner. Don't even say it; I haven't mentioned a word to her about the incident. I simply do not discuss any police matters with my love interests unless they are things that have been made public in the media or the press. It just works best for me."

"I appreciate that, Tony. No problem with your early departure this afternoon. I should do the same and take Ariel out to dinner too. She'll be happy not having to cook tonight. See you bright and early in the morning." The two men shook hands.

⋊

The unmarked Chevy pulled out of the parking lot in San Diego at four-forty-five on Thursday morning, September 26, 1968. Howard Shepherd had no intentions of honking once he arrived at Tony's place. He didn't have to; Tony was waiting for him, small suitcase in hand. He tossed the case in the back of the car and hopped into the passenger seat. "Morning, Chief!"

"Morning, Tony!" Howard Shepherd always remained Chief or Commander to his men; he wasn't stuck up but always believed that a certain degree of respect made for a healthier esprit de corps in the department.

This morning he chose to drive for the first few hours. Having checked with traffic control, he decided on taking highway 101 for most of the trip. Once they hit the outskirts of LA, traffic slowed to a crawl. They were north of LA by ten o'clock and decided it was time to stop for a bite to eat, to check out the men's room, and to change drivers.

Howard Shepherd knew Sergeant Beardsley to be an excellent driver. Had it been anyone else, he would have driven all the way to San Luis Obispo. "Tony, when we get to our destination, let me do all the initial talking. I'll introduce you as my assistant and you will take down any part of the conversation regardless of who is speaking. It will be important to have as complete a record of our interrogation as possible."

"Got it, Chief. I may get to use my rusty shorthand." He jumped into the driver's seat and was pleased finally to be behind the wheel. Tony wasn't exactly what some might have called a good passenger. Once the traffic thinned, he was able to step on the gas. They arrived at Edmond Valley Estates shortly after one o'clock. The gatekeeper stopped them wanting to know who they were trying to visit. Commander Shepherd flashed his police ID, not stating whom they were trying to see; they were admitted without further questioning. They had studied the layout of the ritzy gated community before they left and had no trouble locating 18505 Circular Drive.

A massive wrought iron gate blocked the driveway to the house. Tony jumped out and pressed the doorbell he had spotted right away on the left post of the gate. The response was quick.

"Yes, who is carring, prease?" was the inquiry clearly spoken by an Asian male.

"We are here on official business and wish to speak to Mr. Horatio Alvis III."

"What officiar business do you have with Mr. Arvis?"

"We are from the San Diego police and have urgent business to discuss with him!"

There was dead silence at the other end of the speaker system. "Just moment, prease."

Within seconds the heavy gates swung back, allowing Beardsley to drive through a park-like garden to the front of what most Americans would have referred to as a mansion.

They noticed that the front door was held open as they moved up the right side of an impressive circular stairway. They were greeted by the young Asian man in *livrée*.

"Prease come in; Miss Arvis wirr be light with you."

Shepherd and Beardsley had removed their coats and hats, which were taken by the young man. Minutes later an elegantly dressed Mrs. Alvis approached them. Both men got up.

"I'm Veronica Alvis, the wife of Horatio Alvis III. If Ping, our manservant, understood you correctly, you wish to speak with my husband. He's momentarily out on an errand, but I expect him back shortly."

Shepherd and Beardsley reached for their badges. "I'm Commander Shepherd and this is Sergeant Beardsley, my assistant. We are with the San Diego police and have reason to believe that a boat registered in your husband's name was stranded in our jurisdiction after a horrendous Pacific storm last week. I have asked Sergeant Beardsley to act as a recorder during our investigation. Please be advised that anything you say may be held against you in a court of law. If you feel more comfortable and wish to ask for your lawyer to be present under these circumstances, you may make a call before we commence." Mrs. Alvis sat up straighter in her chair.

"I don't understand. Are we just talking about a stranded little boat that was washed ashore in your waters in San Diego? That craft belonged to my husband long before we were married thirty-five years ago. I've bought him a beautiful and much larger yacht since. The old cutter we gave to our son, Horatio Alvis IV, when he graduated from medical school in 1959. He keeps it in a slip not too distant from our yacht at the Morro Bay Yacht Club—not that he uses it very much; he often speaks of junking it. I'm sure, knowing my son, it was well insured and he will certainly accept any settlement offered by his insurance agent."

"That's a distinct possibility. You have any knowledge why the vessel was baptized *Arabella*— it's sort of an unusual name."

"It was the name of a young woman my husband saw before we were married. He had spoken of having the name scraped off and replaced by a different, more appropriate one to appease me. I told him years ago not to bother and just let Mother Nature take care of things. Guess that's exactly what happened."

A large, black car was turning toward the house and everyone present could detect the unmistakable sound of a garage door opening and closing. Approaching the house more closely, Howard Shepherd realized that the car driven was a Rolls-Royce. Seconds later, Horatio Alvis III stepped into the parlor where the others were seated. "Who are these men and what are they doing here?" was Mr. Alvis's haughty inquiry.

Showing their badges, "I'm Commander Shepherd and this is my colleague, Sergeant Beardsley, from the San Diego police. As we explained to your wife, you may wish to have an attorney present during this investigation. Anything you say may be held against you in a court of law. Your wife has given us some historical background regarding the cutter named *Arabella* bearing the registration HIN #879 47654 0449 in your name. The boat was washed ashore in waters in our jurisdiction after last weekend's horrendous storm. The boat was essentially totally destroyed."

Alvis finally spoke. "That's really too bad. We had no clue where the boat would turn up. Our son called me at the office days ago, informing me that the Morro Bay Yacht Club had contacted him since the boat had apparently been torn away from its moorings and most likely sank during the storm."

Commander Shepherd coughed to clear his throat. "You are saying that neither of you nor your son have been anywhere near the Morro Bay Yacht Club and on either of your vessels during the last week or so?"

"That's correct," said Mr. Alvis III.

"You are absolutely certain, Sir?"

"Yes!"

"Then tell me, who is Juliana A. D. Knecht?"

"I'm not saying another word," said Horatio. He turned to his wife. "Veronica, you better call Max Weinstein. I want Max to be present before this goes any further.

"You may want to wait in your car or make yourselves comfortable. It will take Mr. Weinstein at least thirty minutes before he can be here. For all intents and purposes, he could be in court or otherwise occupied," said Horatio.

Veronica had reached Max Weinstein on her first try; he assured her he would be there as fast as possible.

Chapter 8

VERONICA made the introductions. It was evident that she played the leading role in this matrimonial match. "Max Weinstein, please meet Commander Shepherd and Sergeant Beardsley from the San Diego PD. Apparently Horatio Jr.'s cutter was washed ashore in the San Diego area, totally scuttled according to what we were told. It's still registered in Horatio III's name although our son has been sailing it for years. That's how these gentlemen made the connection to us."

"What's so serious about that? Sounds to me like an insurance claim that could be settled in a relatively simple manner," said Max Weinstein.

Commander Shepherd decided it was high time to open Pandora's box. "It's really not that simple. A young woman was found on the floor of the *Arabella*—and she was dead. A pouch discovered hanging from the back of her waist contained her driver's license, some bills and change amounting to one hundred dollars or less, two keys, a lipstick, and a note. She is now resting in the morgue at our precinct. The autopsy showed that she was poisoned with cyanide. Furthermore,

Juliana Knecht was in her second trimester of pregnancy. The unborn child was a boy."

Veronica gasped. Horatio was staring into space. Max Weinstein realized he needed to speak. "What makes you say she was poisoned? Might this woman, under the circumstances, have committed suicide? I do believe this matter needs indeed further investigation. Who is Juliana A. D. Knecht, anyway? Does the name sound familiar to either of you?" His vision strayed from Veronica to Horatio. Veronica spoke first.

"I've never known anyone by that name; have you Horatio?"

"Yes, I have. I met her at the yacht club about a year ago. Junior introduced her to me. Their paths had crossed in medical school. He had taken her out to dinner once or twice. He told me at the time that Juliana liked sailing and that he had taken her for a sail on a few occasions on the little boat. That's the extent of my knowledge of this woman."

"I believe we need to speak with your son. I recall you telling us earlier that Horatio IV graduated from medical school nine years ago. And he was given possession of the sailboat at that time; is that correct?"

"Yes, that's what I said," confirmed Mrs. Alvis.

"We presume your son no longer lives with you? By the way, how old is he?"

"He was thirty-four in July. And you are correct in your assumption; he no longer lives with us. He's had a bachelor apartment in town for the last four years. He is employed at the Bayside Hospital and practices internal medicine."

"Would he be on duty right now? Under the circumstances, we need to speak with your son ASAP. We have a lot of terri-tory to cover in the next couple of days."

"I believe he is practicing today. When I spoke with him

on the phone last night, he mentioned he had a full roster of patients scheduled," volunteered Horatio III. It was the first time he said anything after Commander Shepherd had dropped the bombshell. He was clearly agitated.

"Don't anyone leave. We'll be back as soon as we have spoken with your son and whoever else." Ping was summoned and returned hats and jackets to the two police officers.

"I won't be able to hang around. I have a late-afternoon appointment with a client. If you feel the need for my presence later, please call me, Veronica," spoke Weinstein.

He shook hands with Shepherd and Beardsley before they got into their respective cars. "Just follow me; I'll point you in the direction to Bayside Hospital," yelled Max Weinstein before he slammed the door of his car.

✕

"Ping, fix me a double scotch on the rocks," ordered Veronica. "And then give Mr. Alvis and me privacy. I don't want to be disturbed unless the San Diego PD honors us with an encore visit. There are tasks for you to do in the kitchen."

The drink, as requested, was set before Veronica promptly. Ping bowed at the waist and backed out of the receiving parlor. Veronica stared at Horatio.

"Let's have it! Or do I need to pull one tooth at a time? Who really is this, Juliana? How come you never mentioned her to me in connection with our son? Is she another of your bimbos you've been shagging behind my back? When you ran for the Senate, you never banked on the media to dig up some of your peccadilloes, or should I have said your darker sides? You know you need my money and me more than I need you.

I could ditch you as fast as you could blink an eye; I've got all the ammunition I want. But I won't make it easy for you; I like being Mrs. Horatio Alvis III. You better learn to live with me, the rich-bitch ice block. I understand that's the endearing name you've bestowed on me in certain social circles of yours. Men are worse at gossiping than women."

"I didn't think anything of it. Juliana was a casual acquaintance of our son. I was pleased to see that he enjoyed some female companionship for a change instead of always having his nose in a book or being deeply involved in some medical research project. His observations of our relationship apparently have turned him completely off the idea of marriage. It wouldn't surprise me at all were he to remain a bachelor."

"That would be a shame; he's such a handsome young man. I just hope he wasn't involved with this Juliana or worse, gotten her pregnant."

"Are we done with this discussion? I would like to get back to my desk."

"Suit yourself. You never can face reality—and anything that goes wrong is always due to my domineering personality."

His back turned, walking away from Veronica, he envisioned Juliana lying dead in the bottom of that miserable cutter. *Why the hell didn't I scrape the name off that damn boat and obliterate the HIN?*

Chapter 9

"THAT'S a perfect parking spot right there, Tony. Let's grab it. Lord knows how long we'll be here. From what Horatio III said, Alvis IV is supposed to have patients lined up the wazoo. This ought to be interesting. I can't wait to see this guy's facial expression when we share with him what we've discovered."

Shepherd and Beardsley walked into the main entrance of the hospital and checked out the directory. Horatio Alvis IV, MD, was shown to have his offices on the second floor in Suite #209. They hopped on the elevator and were facing a receptionist in seconds.

"How may I help you gentlemen? Does either of you have an appointment with Dr. Alvis?"

"Actually, we don't. However, we are here on a personal matter concerning the good doctor. Looking around this rather empty waiting room, might we infer that Dr. Alvis has seen the last of his patients for the day? It is pretty close to closing time according to the posted office hours."

"True, you assumed correctly; he's seeing his last patient for the day right now. May I tell him what this is all about? I'm not used to letting patients into his offices who are neither scheduled nor properly registered with us."

"That won't be necessary. We'll present our credentials in private." The receptionist, Ms. Done, as the sign said on her desk, was indeed done in. She stared at her appointment calendar, obviously not believing what was happening.

As the last patient emerged from the examining room, Ms. Done rose from her seat immediately. Before she could say anything, Commander Shepherd flashed his San Diego PD badge directly behind her. The doctor took the hint.

"Thank you, Ms. Done. You may leave for the day. I'll close up after I see these gentlemen out." Done was completely undone and not sure how to handle the situation. It was something that had never occurred before. *Who are these guys? What do they have on him? Are they representing some group of undesirables? Is he gay? Gosh, I don't know what to make of this!* She grabbed her purse from the bottom drawer of her desk, slammed the desk shut and locked it, extinguished the light on her desk lamp by pushing a handy button, and stormed out of the office. She mumbled some expletives heading for her car in the parking garage, still shaking her head in disbelief.

"Come in, gentlemen. Actually, I was expecting you. My mother called me on my private line; however, she didn't tell me what this is all about." Shepherd extended his right hand to Dr. Alvis. "I'm Commander Shepherd and this is my assistant, Sergeant Beardsley. We are from the San Diego PD. As we advised your mother and father, anything you say to us will be duly recorded by Sergeant Beardsley and may be held against you in a court of law. Your mother and father eventually asked Max Weinstein to join us in the questioning of them regarding the matter of concern to us. We don't know if Mr.

Weinstein is your legal counsel, or if you wish to call whoever does represent you in such situations. We certainly have the time to wait."

"Why would I need legal counsel? I've done nothing wrong and I have nothing to hide. Shoot! What'ya got?"

"What brings us here is the stranding of that old cutter your parents gave you as a graduation present from medical school nine years ago. You must really like sailing that old thing to even consider it a suitable present from parents obviously as wealthy as yours appear to be. But that's neither here nor there. Your father told us that you were contacted by the Morro Bay Yacht Club. It was speculated that the boat was torn away from its moorings on the weekend of the dreadful storm. I understand the brunt of it occurred here five days ago. That would make it last Sunday. Where were you last Sunday? Can you account for your time?"

"Wait a minute, there must be more to this than my stranded sailboat. What the hell is going on? Let me look at my calendar. As I said, I have nothing to hide. I slept in late, had breakfast in my apartment, went for a run for a good hour, and then took a much-needed shower. I swung by the hospital to catch up on some paperwork. I was in this office from about one until five-ish. Staff on duty could clearly vouch for me, although many chose not to come in because of the increasing winds. Normally, I grab a bite to eat for lunch at one of the little bistros near here. However, on Sunday, because of all that rain and hail, I stayed in and had some of the delectable hospital fare. People must have seen me in the cafeteria.

"When one of the nurses on duty whistled retreat shortly after five, I called a buddy of mine to meet me at the *Cat & Mouse* pub to shoot the breeze over a couple brews and a light supper. I hate eating alone. Dr. Matt Lawler has been a good friend since high school. We graduated from different medical schools but always remained in close touch. He dropped me off at my pad close to ten o'clock. I set my alarm after I entered my apartment, took another shower, and went straight to bed. I left for my office at seven-thirty in the morning. All cars entering and leaving our underground garage are monitored by a gatekeeper. I received the call from the Morro Bay Yacht Club just before noon on Monday. Whoever I spoke to was positive that the moorings were torn by the high winds that pounded the waters. That's all I have to say. Does that answer your questions?"

"Obviously, nursing staff on Sunday duty, Dr. Lawler, and the gatekeeper at your apartment building will be able to corroborate your accounting of what you did and where you did it on the Sunday in question. I believe it is time for us to share with you why we came all the way from San Diego to investigate a possible crime. The person who located the scuttled boat on the beach also discovered a body lying on the floor in the back of the hull.

"When my colleagues and I were called to investigate, we found the corpse of a young woman in the back area of the chamber just beyond the bulkhead. When moving her onto a stretcher, we noticed a pouch suspended in the back of her waist. Before the coroner performed the autopsy, he examined the contents of the pouch which, among other things, included a driver's license revealing the identity of the dead woman. The staff photographer produced these close-up photographs of the deceased."

Shepherd realized immediately that Alvis Jr. knew who he was looking at. *"Oh, my God,* it's Juliana Arabella. I can't believe what I'm seeing. Was she hurt during the storm? Was she struck during the destruction of the craft? I don't understand!"

"No, she wasn't hurt by anything structurally from the boat or by wind and water. The autopsy revealed that she ingested cyanide. The vial was clutched tightly in her right hand.

"Your father implied that you had seen Ms. Knecht a while ago but did not actually date her regularly. Do you recall when you saw her last?"

"Actually, I do. I was leaving church after Epiphany services. That would make it January sixth of this year. I wasn't even aware that she attended my church. We stopped at a Subway and grabbed a quick bite to eat. We talked perhaps for an hour. She told me she was seeing a man who was several years older than she, and jokingly mentioned the man was perhaps old enough to be her father. I wished her the best as we parted. That was the last time I saw Juliana Arabella."

"You haven't heard the rest. The autopsy showed further that Juliana was in her second trimester of pregnancy and that the fetus was a vital male."

Young Horatio scratched his scalp. "I can't fathom what you are telling me. Have you tried to find Juliana's mother? She's a widow. Her husband died many years ago. From what I remember, Mrs. Knecht raised Juliana pretty much on her own. Fortunately, her deceased husband left her well off enough to afford Juliana a decent education. That's how we met at first. She was studying pharmacology when I was pursuing internal medicine. Don't get me wrong. I liked Juliana very much but wasn't interested in a serious relationship. Besides that, observing the "marital bliss" in my own home was not exactly encouraging me to follow in my parents' footsteps."

"Thanks, young man, if I may call you that, doctor. Would you mind giving us any information you may have regarding Juliana's mother, specifically her address and perhaps a telephone number?"

"Her name is Arabella Davos Knecht, and she lives at 4700 Main Blvd. I'm sorry to say I do not have her telephone number. When Juliana and I met serendipitously after medical school, she was living by herself in an apartment in LA. She invited me twice to have dinner with her and her mother. That's how I happen to know where Mrs. Knecht lives and that she is a widow. I suppose she would be listed in the local directory. She didn't strike me as being secretive."

"We'll let you go for now. Somehow, I trust you. It's a gut feeling. Sorry to have kept you so long and to have been the bearer of such shocking news. Don't leave town. We may have further questions for you. We recommend you be guarded in sharing with your parents what you discussed with us." Shepherd and Beardsley shook hands with Dr. Alvis and let themselves out of the offices.

Chapter 10

"WE crossed Main Boulevard earlier. I have a pretty good sense where it is," said Beardsley after he made a wheelie.

"I know it's after six o'clock and my stomach is hanging at half mast. I'm sure yours can't be in much better shape. It's been a long day since breakfast," was Shepherd's assessment of the situation. "Let's get this over with; it's probably the hardest thing we'll have to do today. I hate telling a parent their kid is dead. I'll keep watching for house numbers. We can't be too far from 4700. Yup, there it is, and I see there's a light on in the room that faces the street. Let's go for it!"

It was a small house but very well kept. Plantings in front were impressive. Beardsley pressed the button for the doorbell. A kindly face answered the summons promptly. The woman was perhaps in her late fifties, possibly early sixties. Her hair was snow white, cut in a fashionable bob, and swept back on the left side. Mrs. Knecht greeted the two strangers with a big smile. "Are you lost, gentlemen? I don't recall ever seeing you in the neighborhood. You are not trying to sell me anything, are you?"

"No, indeed. We are with the San Diego PD and here on official business." Both flashed their police badges.

"Please come in; I don't like to stand under my door and talk to people. Also, I would much prefer to sit in my parlor and speak with you. Now tell me, what's this all about?"

"I'm Commander Shepherd and this is my colleague, Sergeant Beardsley. We have some questions for you and then will explain why we are calling on you at this late hour. Our visit concerns your daughter Juliana. When was the last time you saw her or spoke with her?"

"Oh, no! Is there anything wrong with my girl? Did you say you were from San Diego?"

"Yes we are; perhaps you didn't understand. We are with the San Diego police."

"Juliana was here about ten days ago, two weeks ago at the most. I thought she had put on a little weight but didn't comment on it since she was always so concerned about keeping her girlish figure. We had so much fun that night looking through a box of old photographs. She's always been such a curious girl. At one point, we came across a photo of a young man. She kept staring at it and insisted on my telling her who it was. It was a man I dated quite seriously before I left San Luis Obispo and moved to an apartment in Los Angeles. I'd hoped to make it into the movies but was never picked up."

Arabella Knecht continued. "Soon it was my turn to be curious; I was holding a photograph of a young girl walking hand-in-hand with Juliana out of the high school building in Glendale, where we used to live before I moved back to San Luis Obispo. Juliana couldn't believe the puzzled look on my face. 'Mom, you must be joking. How could you forget her? That is my best friend, Ulrike Hammer. We sat next to each other ever since junior high, attended the same classes in med school, and still are the best of friends. She looks slightly different today, after all the plastic surgery she needed done after the burns she received in that awful fire in the Kern's Department Store. It's been at least three years since she had all that work done on her face. Sadly to say, that tragedy not only changed her appearance, but she has become a recluse and suffers from extreme bouts of depression. Are you sure you don't remember her at all?'

"Of course, I remembered her as an adult after the surgical intervention, but for the life of me I couldn't put a name to that girl in the high school photo."

Commander Shepherd looked across the room at Beardsley. He read the message loud and clear. "Mrs. Knecht, to come back to my earlier question. Do you recall when you last spoke with Juliana; I presume you stay in touch by phone regularly?"

"Yes, yes, of course. If I'm not mistaken, we talked last on Friday night. She sounded somewhat down when I called her. When I questioned her, she told me she was just fine—perhaps a little less bubbly than I'm used to, but I detected nothing in her voice that caused me to be alarmed. All of us have a down day now and then." She could see the frown on Shepherd's face.

"Please tell me my Juliana is OK."

"Unfortunately, that is not the case. There is no other way to say it. We are terribly sad to share this with you, but your beautiful Juliana is no longer with us on this earth." Mrs. Knecht gasped as her hands covered her face. For a moment Shepherd thought she was going to faint.

"Oh, NO! NO! NO! You can't be talking about my Juliana Arabella. She can't be gone."

Commander Shepherd stood up and put his arms around the poor woman, trying to show his empathy. She was inconsolable and sobbed bitterly.

"Now I've lost everything. She was my one and only joy in life after my husband passed away. He was so good to her and always loved her as if she had been his own."

Shepherd was taken aback. He looked at her with his big brown eyes. Arabella realized she had said something she shouldn't have revealed to a total stranger, worse, to a police officer. "Don't be afraid to tell us anything that could help us solve the mystery. You are not on trial here. Again, we are so sad to be the bearers of such tragic news." He held her firmly in his strong arms.

"Yes, I had Juliana out of wedlock when I was twenty-three. I moved to Los Angeles after I discovered I was with child. I met Anton at a dance when Juliana wasn't quite two years old. He insisted on legally adopting her and was proud to call Juliana his daughter. My parents never knew that Juliana wasn't Anton's offspring. I shared with my family that I was marrying a widower with a child—and they bought it.

"When she was ten years old, we told Juliana that Anton was not her father. She never cared to know who her biological father was. Juliana wanted to honor me by including the initial of my maiden name, Davos, in hers. After she graduated from high school, she always insisted on being known as Juliana A. D. Knecht. Anton Knecht was a wonderful man, husband, and father."

"We are very much saddened about your loss of Juliana. It would appear she was surprised by last Sunday's terrifying storm. We believe she was trying to see someone at the Morro

Bay Yacht Club and eventually sought shelter on one of the boats in the harbor. Mind you this is all speculation. No one seems to know what really happened. One of the boats, a cutter belonging to Dr. Horatio Alvis III, was missing on Monday. It was surmised that it was taken out to sea by the horrendous winds that prevailed. Does this make any sense to you?" By the mere mention of the Alvis name, the mien of her face turned angry.

"No, no, this just cannot be. I know of the yacht club. She told me once that she had met the young Horatio Alvis in med school. She didn't really date him, but they shared a few meals and he took her out on his boat several times. He actually taught her how to sail the cutter at her insistence. For some unknown reason, sailing was in her blood.

"As a matter of fact, he had dinner with us in this very house on two occasions. When his father ran for political office and there was some negative publicity in the papers, I pleaded with Juliana to stop seeing the young doctor. I thought she could do better than that. I know his folks have a lot of money, but that wasn't what Juliana needed. She deserved a loving man. Perhaps young Alvis could have given her that. But I wanted to be sure." *I didn't want history to repeat itself, and far worse,* she thought.

"Sorry to say, we have not shared all there is to this story with you. The Alvis boat was washed ashore in San Diego a few days later. The boat was basically destroyed. Both masts had been toppled, and it is a miracle that the *Arabella* didn't sink. Juliana's body was found on the floor of the boat. She had identification, money, keys, a lipstick, and a typed note in a small pouch she was wearing. Needless to say, an autopsy had to be performed. Juliana was in her second trimester of pregnancy; she was carrying a little boy. More tragically, it is speculated that Juliana took her own life by ingesting cyanide, a most deadly poison."

Arabella almost collapsed into the commander's arms. She screamed: *"This can't be true. My Juliana was a good Christian; she would never have taken her own life or killed a child she was carrying. I raised her to be more responsible than that. NO! NO! NO! This can't be true. I demand there be an inquest!"* Arabella was torn like a dead tree in a windstorm.

Commander Shepherd looked into Arabella's eyes, the eyes of a tragically hurt mother. "Be assured there will be an inquest, and we shall get to the bottom of this. Personally, I do not want to believe Juliana took her own life. It will have to be proven forensically, and whoever was responsible for Juliana Arabella's death will meet his fate in a court of law." He pulled back the sleeve of his jacket with care, giving his watch a quick glance. He wasn't quite confidant how to pave their way to a suitable exit.

"Now, can we make you a cup of tea or call a neighbor or someone to spend time with you? We absolutely hate to leave you alone after the shocking news we had to impart to you. I'm married and have a daughter and don't know how I would deal with the death of my child were that ever to happen."

Arabella reached up to the commander's face and touched it gently. "Thank you for holding me while you gave me such awful news about my beautiful girl. I could tell how difficult it was for you to let me know. My next-door neighbor is a widow just like I am; she was childless and always loved Juliana. She'll be good company. We'll cry together over a cup of tea. You men go now. It's been a long and challenging day for you. It cannot be easy to have a job like yours. I feel for you and I feel for myself. Just go. I'll be OK in a while. I'll say a prayer for my Juliana and for you. God bless you." Her eyes were flooded with tears.

"Please call your neighbor before we leave. We cannot just leave you alone."

Arabella dialed her neighbor's number and asked her to be with her for a while. "Just come, I'll tell you all about it when you get here. Come right away. I have two kind gentlemen who are anxious to leave. They must be starving. If I understood correctly, they haven't eaten since breakfast."

"I'm on my way. Don't fret. I'll bring Freddy for company. I know you love the way he purrs."

"Thanks again for being so kind," said Arabella Knecht to the departing officers. "Doris, Freddy, and I will mourn Juliana appropriately." She practically shooed them out the door. Perhaps she wanted to spare them having to tell the sad story one more time.

Chapter II

"DID you spot the Italian restaurant on the corner as I pulled up to Mrs. Knecht's house?"

"Darn tootin'; I've been secretly salivating over a hunk of lasagna. I felt terrible when things got so quiet now and then. My growling tummy was almost embarrassing. Let's not waste any more time searching for anything fancier," belched Howard Shepherd.

"I know what I'm having. I'm ordering the biggest, most heavily loaded pizza in the joint—stuffed crust and all. I'm ready to eat a horse and chase the rider," was Tony's assessment.

"Our hotel is in this neighborhood and you are driving, Chief. I'll pull myself a couple of Pabsts, if you don't mind."

"I'll have one myself with that lasagna. I can already taste it. And cut out that "Chief Crap" for God's sake. I know it's my idea when we are on duty; right now all I want to be is just your very hungry and thirsty buddy."

They stepped into Rick's Trattoria, and the smells of basil and oregano hit their nostrils. "Look at this classy joint. I love walking into a place, hearing someone tickle those ivories with a touch of class," said Howard.

"Follow me, gentlemen. I couldn't help overhearing you commenting on our piano player. Pavlov is a find. I'll seat you at this table, not too far from the action." As Pavlov was finishing a rendition of the "Meditation" from *Thais,* a guy at a neighboring table requested "If You Were the Only Girl in the World." Listening to the song, Howard looked up at Tony; his eyes were brimming with tears.

"What's wrong, Howard?"

"I used to play and sing that song for Ariel. I cannot get the images of Juliana and Arabella out of my mind. We've got to find that bastard who's responsible for this villainous act."

"We will; we will, Howard. But for the moment, let's get something in our stomachs in short order. I may even snatch a bite from your lasagna while I wait to get ahold of that pizza of mine. That will take a few minutes. In the meantime, I'll have breadsticks with my salad and enjoy that first Pabst. It'll slide down real easy."

The waiter smiled; he loved it when people came into Rick's with a good appetite. "Two Pabsts coming up right away, gentlemen. Salads and sticks to follow promptly. You'll love our lasagna, Sir. I'll get you that second Pabst while they are twirling that pizza for you in the kitchen," said Enrico, their humming waiter.

"I hate to bring up business, Tony. First thing in the morning, I want to head down to Morro Bay and check out that yacht club. I want to talk to the harbormaster and the head honcho at the club. Once we are done there, I'm aiming for an encore visit to the fancy mansion. I dunno why, but that

Horatio Alvis III rubbed me the wrong way. There's more to this than meets the eye."

"I agree, Howard. I'm with you all the way on that one. Here comes your lasagna. *Enjoy it!* If you don't object, I'll have a fork or two. I'll let you have some of that *gigondo* pizza I ordered; as hungry as I am, I'll never be able to put it away by myself." Tony burped, covering his mouth. "Sorry, I must have drank that too rapidly." He was thankful for the musical cover-up.

When they left Rick's, neither was feeling any pains. Howard had a couple of Rusty Nails after dessert. "I'm glad I only have to drive a few deserted blocks to get near a bed. This has been one hell of a day. Here, let me hold on to you, Tony. Are you as snockered as am I?"

"Remember, I had five Pabsts to your one. Of course, those Rusty Nails did the finishing touch on you. Brrrrrurp! Sorry, boss. You better handle those wheels."

They walked into the Old Main Hotel and were checked in quickly. Tony stripped down to his boxers and hit the mattress. Howard got naked and jumped into the shower. As the hot water eased the pain in his shoulders and neck, he began to hum and then sang softly: "If you were the only girl in the world and I were the only boy." He was thankful for the powerful stream of hot water disguising the tears running down his face. Streams of water could disguise his tears but not the images that floated through his mind.

Chapter 12

BY eight o'clock the guys had finished a good breakfast, confirmed another night's stay with the concierge, and were headed for the dirty Chevy parked in the underground. "Boy, was I glad there was lots of parking space when I pulled in last night. I wouldn't have wanted to park too touchy to any other vehicles. Man, those Rusty Nails surely did their job. Well, Tony, you slept like a log as soon as you hit those pillows. Be thankful for your snoring, you didn't hear me serenade in the shower. Hopefully the walls in this joint are thick enough and no one else heard me either." Howard was glad Tony had offered to drive this morning.

Howard Shepherd and Tony Beardsley arrived at the Morro Bay Yacht Club less than two hours later. They had enjoyed the ride through the wine country, seeing so many colorfully dressed Mexicans harvesting what would become the 1968

vintage. "Pull in right here. Let's hope the harbormaster is in this early."

"What'ya mean early, Chief? It's after ten o'clock; he ought to be on the job." Walking into the lobby, they became immediately aware of the rich woods used in the creation of the facility and the masculine touches in furniture and the décor selected. "Nice place," said Tony. "That must be his office; the sign says: Gerald Smothers, Harbormaster."

Howard used the brass door knocker, hitting the heavily carved ebony door firmly. "Come in, please!" was their signal to enter. Gerald Smothers rose from his leather swivel chair and extended his right hand toward Commander Shepherd. "Gerald Smothers!"

Shaking his hand, Howard introduced himself and Tony; both men flashed their San Diego PD badges. "What brings you to our part of the state?" inquired the harbormaster.

"We are investigating a possible crime. A sailboat that was said to have been harbored at the Morro Bay Yacht Club was stranded on a beach in San Diego on September 24. We are interested in learning what the conditions were like in your area on Sunday, September 22."

"It was a horrific storm out of the West; we had twenty- to thirty-foot waves, pouring rain, and damaging hail. The harbor was a disaster. If you look around, you'll see many a small vessel still thrown ashore. Many of our boat owners reside in distant places and aren't even aware of the damage that might have been done to their properties. The place is teeming with insurance agents scrambling to settle with their respective clients.

"It was one of the worst days and nights I recall since becoming Harbormaster forty years ago. It's almost time for me to consider retiring. Commodore Ari Konstantinopolis at the yacht club and I started working here at about the same time. Lately, he and I are jokingly discussing what we shall do once we are retired. They'll give us the boot for sure when we hit that seventy mark."

"Well, you're not quite there yet. That information you gave us was very helpful. We won't take more of your time. We'll head over to the club and hopefully can touch base with the Commodore. He may shed some light on the situation. Thanks again for your valuable input."

They shook hands with Gerald Smothers and walked over to the Morro Bay Yacht Club. After sitting in the car for almost two hours, a little stroll in the fresh morning breeze did them good. "Perfect morning, Tony. Did you notice how many slips are empty? They can't possibly be all out at sea. What I notice are mostly large yachts and good-sized sailing vessels."

"Maybe some of the small stuff we witnessed along the shore was torn from these slips. Well, let's get the dope from the Commodore," said Beardsley. A liveried young man opened the door as they approached the club.

"We are looking for Commodore Ari Konstantinopolis. Might he be in and available to speak with us? We are with the San Diego PD," spoke Shepherd.

"Follow me; I'll take you directly to his office." He knocked on the door and opened it as soon as he was given the word to enter. Commodore Ari Konstantinopolis stood up to greet his visitors in a most friendly manner.

"Commodore Ari Konstantinopolis; make it Ari, that's just too much of a tongue twister for most people."

"I'm Commander Howard Shepherd and this fine man is my colleague, Sergeant Tony Beardsley, representing the San

Diego PD, precinct #18. We are here on a mission and would appreciate your input." He related some of the San Diego findings and then pulled from his file folder the retouched and enlarged photo taken from Juliana's driver's license, placing it on Konstantinopolis's desk. "Have you ever seen or known this woman?"

Ari Konstantinopolis winced. "Yes, I've seen the young woman on several occasions. Quite a number of years ago—don't ask me exactly what year—I saw this woman palling around with young Horatio Alvis. I saw them together in our dining room; and on other occasions, he was showing her how to sail the craft that is now in question. Of course, his father's yacht is another story. After his wife bought him that fabulous vessel—you see it right over there—many years ago, he paid little attention to the old cutter. He gave it to his son as a present. I've often been tempted to tell father and son to do something about the appearance of that old pot. One time I took heart and spoke up. After Horatio Sr. told me not to bother him with such trivia, I gave up on it. The sailboat was moored close to the harbor entrance and not seen by too many regular visitors.

"I didn't mean to deviate from your inquiry; I saw the young lady in question on a few occasions earlier this year in the company of Horatio Sr. Apparently, he entertained her for dinner on his yacht, the *Horatio III*. I'm not divulging any secrets; during his unsuccessful run for the US Senate, there was much in the media about the philandering of Mr. Horatio Alvis III. Reporters were constantly trying to catch him with one blond or red-haired bimbo of the day. I'm surprised Veronica hasn't gotten rid of him yet. I never understood what she saw in him. He was piss-poor and she was a class act in social circles. She must've been impressed by his name."

Commander Shepherd just nodded. "Tony, did you get all of that? Very interesting, very interesting indeed. I have a few more questions for you. Were you the person who contacted young Horatio regarding the missing cutter? Is it really possible for that boat to be torn from its moorings?

"You don't by any chance recall seeing the young woman or either Horatio Senior or Junior at the yacht club last Sunday?"

"Well, let me answer your questions in order. I'm not accustomed to being fired at with so many questions at one time. Yes, I called Dr. Horatio Alvis IV later on Monday morning and reported the lost vessel. And yes, it is a good possibility that the moorings were torn by the storm. It probably would not have happened had the boat been located closer to the inner harbor. Where it was, there was full impact from wind and the high seas. I'm amazed that she made it all the way to San Diego and didn't sink.

"Regarding your final question, I'm sorry to say I did not lay eyes on any of the three on that day. It was utter pandemonium in this place trying to save as many vessels as possible from the storm. Most people who were present that day were disguised with face protectors, scarves, and bulky jackets and wraps. All of us were glad we survived the tempest in as good a shape as we did. Only the next day did we become aware how many smaller boats had been impacted by the disturbance. I would have loved to tell you I saw that infidel in action, but I didn't."

Howard winked at Tony, conveying that he considered the interview concluded. All three men got up and shook hands. "Thank you for being so cooperative and forthcoming. Be forewarned: If there should be an inquest and possibly even a trial in San Diego, you may be summoned to testify. Thank you again!"

"I fully understand. It will be an honor to help you in solving this matter. Let me see you out. I can stand a touch of fresh air. I'm not the office type. With my heritage, I'm a man of sea and wind. Great meeting you!" They smiled at each other before parting and going their separate ways.

Chapter 13

"OK, Tony. Now for the coup de grace. I want a chat with Mr. Horatio Alvis III before we end this sojourn north. I have no intentions of driving back to San Diego later today. Let's enjoy another great meal and the entertainment at Rick's before we get a good-night's sleep. It will make that long drive home tomorrow easier to digest. Agree?"

"You're the boss. Let me drive; I've gotten an excellent feel for this area by now. You just sit back and enjoy the pretty sights. I love the looks of the wine country, especially this time of year with the harvest in full swing. I've no idea how they would ever get all of these jobs done without the many helping hands reaching out from the south. I saw a nice little roadside café on the outskirts of San Luis Obispo. Let's stop for a bite before we tackle Alvis III. I never again want to be as famished as I was last night. That just about did me in."

"You're not just a-kiddin'; I know exactly what you mean. I'm all in favor of stopping."

It was shortly after one o'clock when Tony wheeled into

the parking lot at Rosalinda's Café. The pretty young hostess guided them to a pleasant booth. "Would you care for a drink?"

"Normally, we would. However, duty calls. Lemon water will do just fine."

"I can recommend our spectacular chicken salad on a freshly baked croissant accompanied by pears and dates. You'll love it. Be adventurous; try something other than boring burgers, although, those we serve here aren't what'ya might call boring. What'll it be?"

"You sold us on the croissants. Sounds terrific."

"The fresh cashews, pecans, and new green grapes not only give a lovely crunch to the salad but really surprise your taste buds. Good choice! Are you sure I can't talk you into a glass of our very best Chardonnay?"

"Would love it but we are on a mission. Thanks anyway."

As soon as the charmer had moved away, Howard grinned at Tony. "Whenever someone mentions 'cashews' it takes me back to a very dear Jewish friend. Both of her daughters married Catholics. She always referred to her grandchildren as "my little Cashews." The inventiveness of the English language cracks me up. Well, here come our salads. I'm already salivating."

After the first bite, they said in one voice, *"Wonderful!"*

Hopping back into the Chevy, Howard voiced: "Now I can handle what is to come."

⋈

They had no problems getting past the gatekeeper. Howard jumped out of the car as Tony pulled up once more in front of the impressive wrought iron gate at the Alvis mansion. Of course, Ping answered the call. "Just moment, prease. Check with Missus." And as if by magic, the gate opened. They noticed the car Alvis III had driven the day before. "That must mean he is home," Howard observed, motioning to Tony by moving his right shoulder in the direction of the parked black Rolls-Royce.

Ping ushered them into the receiving parlor. "Missus and Mistur wirr be with you light away!" He giggled and bowed, backing out of the room after taking their hats. "Thanks, we'll keep our jackets!" said the Commander.

Veronica made her grand entrance. She was a stunning woman in her early sixties. A well-maintained figure, makeup, and bottled magic had done their tricks. Of course, heels and designer clothes didn't hurt the cause either. "Welcome, gentlemen. How have your inquiries gone? Are you wiser today than you were yesterday?"

"Actually we've made some interesting discoveries, none of which we are able to share with you at this time. I presume, you understand?" asked Howard Shepherd. We would like to speak with your husband in private, if you don't have any objections?"

"None at all. Knowing him, he'll probably prefer to have further discussions with you in Max Weinstein's presence. But I'll let him make that call." She picked up a brass bell and rang for Ping to reappear.

"Please take these gentlemen to my husband's office."

Ping bowed deeply. "Prease forrow me." He knocked lightly and then opened the door, not having waited for any invitation for the visitors to enter. Horatio Alvis had his back to the door. He must have known who entered his very private space. Before he turned around with a quick swivel of the sizable leather chair, Commander Shepherd spoke with excitement in his voice. "Is that one of the few classic old Remington Rands still in existence? I remember my grandfather typing on one of those. May I look at it more closely? Does she still work?"

Horatio was totally taken off guard and impressed that one of these lowly police officers could actually appreciate something in his elaborate office, something as ordinary as an old typewriter. He grabbed a fresh piece of paper from the second drawer of his desk and inserted it into the machine. "Of course, it still works. Let me show you. What's that sentence they always have you type in typing school?"

"Oh, I remember: *The quick brown fox jumps over the lazy dog,*" volunteered Shepherd.

Horatio typed it quickly and yanked it expertly from the old Remington Rand. Before he could do anything else with it, Howard Shepherd saw an opportunity. "Do me a big favor; fold it carefully and put it in one of those envelopes you have on your desktop—and please seal it. I want nothing to happen to it between here and the time we get back to San Diego. My wife is a historian; she'll treasure this piece of paper forever. I should take a picture of the Remington. You mind?" Before Alvis could object, he had snapped a few shots with the handy little Leica he always carried.

"Thank you so much. I know this has nothing to do with us being here, but I was so taken by that ancient machine. It's wonderful that it is so well preserved and still in great functioning order. So many people today believe in 'new and improved' but not necessarily 'better.'"

Horatio did exactly as told and handed the sealed envelope to Commander Shepherd, who put it carefully into his left breast pocket of his suit jacket. Tony Beardsley almost wet his pants. He couldn't believe what the old fox had just succeeded in doing.

"Thank you again, Mr. Alvis. But now to some serious matters. We have interviewed your son; a Mrs. Knecht, the mother of Juliana; the harbormaster at Morro Bay; and spoke with Commodore Ari Konstantinopolis, the CEO of the Morro Bay Yacht Club. One of the hardest things we had to do was to advise Mrs. Knecht of the death of her daughter.

"Your son pretty much corroborated what you and your wife shared with us yesterday. The harbormaster painted a vivid picture of what went on during the storm last Sunday, and Commodore Konstantinopolis confirmed what we suspected. It seems almost certain that the boat was torn away from the moorings by the hurricane winds and was washed out to sea. Both he and the harbormaster cannot believe that the vessel survived the storm and didn't sink. So, for all intents and purposes, we actually didn't learn very much that is new.

"I do have to ask you one more time in front of my assistant. Is it true you did not see and/or have any dealings with Juliana A. D. Knecht last Sunday? As a matter of fact, can you tell us where you were Sunday night?"

"Again, I have not seen this woman since sometime earlier this year; it may have been even last year. Last Sunday, I *was* in Morro Bay and had dinner with an old friend of mine. We met in college and have remained lifelong friends; he's a widower and lives by himself. Unfortunately, he's in the early stages of senile dementia, and I see him regularly on weekends in Morro Bay. It's a very sad and depressing situation. Nevertheless, I feel obliged to see him as often as possible.

"We had cocktails at five. These days I have to fix

his favorite—Old Fashioneds. He can't remember all the ingredients. I usually take him a couple of steaks and fix them on his grill. Having a decent meal now and then and having me there to listen to his old stories gives him something to look forward to. I left his house about nine o'clock or nine-thirty-ish. It was still storming unbelievably. I almost took him up on his offer to sleep in his guest bedroom. It was an awful ride home; but I wanted to make sure things were OK with Veronica and the house. Not to worry; all was just fine around here. The cyclone had its greatest impact near the coast. Does that answer your questions? I don't know what else to tell you. I suppose Max should have been here. Moreover, I have nothing to hide."

"OK, Mr. Alvis. We've gone as far as we can. May I suggest that you not leave San Luis Obispo for anything extensive, and certainly not any out-of-the-country-type travel, until we've advised you that you are in the clear. We have much further to go. There may be an official inquest and perhaps a trial in San Diego down the road. We want you to be prepared and be available for any legal action in which you might be involved. Do you understand what I'm telling you?"

Horatio nodded.

"You need to affirm with your voice for the recording secretary."

"Yes, I do understand."

"We'll take our leave now. I hope we never have to meet again, certainly not under such circumstances." Both men exited Alvis's office without shaking hands with their host. That was telling.

Ping was summoned and asked to see the Commander and the Sergeant to their car. They did not notice Veronica watching the goings-on from the balcony of her bedroom. She stormed downstairs as soon as she saw the old Chevy pass through the open gate.

⋈

"Well, what did you learn? What did they ask you? Are they coming back? I need to know. I'm surprised they didn't arrest you! Lord knows I may have to withdraw huge sums from holdings to bail you out of jail. Answer me. Don't just sit there like a bump on a log!"

"They told me that all we shared with them yesterday checked out with our son and the individuals they spoke to at Morro Bay. I did tell them about my visit with Ernest last Sunday. It might be tough to challenge my alibi—all things considered."

"What do you mean by alibi? That's all you did while you were in Morro Bay, or isn't it? Don't tell me you had another rendezvous at the *Horatio III* with one of your bimbos. Answer me!"

"Honest to God, the way you talk and always accuse me of things. They warned me not to leave town for anything until a possible inquest or trial in San Diego is over. They implied that they have barely scratched the surface of the investigation. That's about it."

"You mean to say that's all that transpired in your office? I just cannot believe this. I should have listened in. Live and learn. I'll have Ping fix me my favorite poison; I'll need it tonight." She walked out of Horatio's office and slammed the door hard.

X

As soon as the wrought iron gate closed behind them, Tony burst out laughing. "How the hell did you ever come up with that brilliant idea about the Remington Rand typewriter? It was classic Sherlock Holmes. I almost wet my pants watching the whole maneuver. He fell for it hook, line, and sinker. Now I can't wait to get back to the precinct and compare the two documents. *And let's be very careful about the fingerprints.* What a coup! You are amazing. I'll change my name to Mr. Watson."

"Hold on. Was I that convincing? Actually, Ariel will love the photos; the paper she can't have for now. If it turns out the way I imagined the whole scenario, that will become a key piece of evidence. I'm proud of what we achieved in these two days. But you know what, I'm ready for a drink and some good Italian cuisine. And furthermore, I'm tickled you wanted to stop at Rosalinda's Café. Those croissants hit the spot."

As they walked into Rick's Italian Trattoria, Pavlov was intoning "As Time Goes By." Howard smiled. "You are probably too young to appreciate 'Casablanca' as much as I do. Takes me right back. I was a kid when it first appeared on the silver screen, but have I loved that story from the day I first saw it. Black and white and all. "But on to more urgent matters; tonight I'll start off with a Rusty Nail and have some Pinot Noir with my dinner. What appeals to you Tony?"

"Of course, I have to down a few Pabsts. Other than the great salad and sticks, I'll have Fettuccine Alfredo. I'll top it off with that fabulous banana cheesecake they are featuring tonight. I had that once in the Galapagos Islands.

"What tickles your fancy other than the Rusty Nail? And

watch out for them Rusty Nails—they'll go down real easy, almost easier than my Pabsts."

"Don't remind me. I remember well from last night. I think I'll have the salad and sticks and Veal Parmigiana. I'll give the Pinot Noir a whirl. That dessert you are talking about sounds great. Never have had it. I'm game to try new things, like collecting writing samples composed on old Remington Rand typewriters."

Tony cracked up. "Maybe Pavlov can come up with a song. I've never heard what he is playing right now. You know it, Howard?"

"It's the theme song from *Now Voyager*. You are not old enough to appreciate that famous last line spoken by no other than the incomparable Bette Davis: *'Oh Jerry, don't let's ask for the moon. We have the stars.'*"

"Gosh, Howard, I had no idea you were such a movie buff."

"My mom loved the movies. She dragged me along for company and I got hooked. You can't beat some of those golden oldies," was Howard's come back.

Chapter 14

COMMANDER Shepherd settled the hotel bill after their celebration dinner at Rick's. Both he and Tony decided to shower and pack at night, making a very early departure for San Diego a possibility. "I'm pleased you saw it my way to get on the road at six o'clock. I hate driving in total darkness, but I want to put LA behind us as early as possible. It will help not having to deal with weekday traffic."

Counting their blessings, they were having breakfast south of LA at nine-thirty. "We made good time, and I expect to be at our offices no later than one o'clock. With a bit of good luck, Coroner Fortran will be at the office. I realize it is Saturday, and if it's been a slow week, he may have chosen not to show. In that case, I'll call him as soon as we arrive. I know he will want to learn what happened during our two-day investigation."

❉

Walking into his office, Commander Shepherd spotted

right away that part of his unsightly desk had been rearranged by Alice Walker to make room for several special deliveries received from Ms. Drew at the San Luis Obispo Public Library. He just gave the thick envelopes a cursory glance for now and dialed Archibald Fortran's home number.

"Fortran residence, Myra speaking."

"Hello, Myra. Howard Shepherd. Is Archibald by any chance home?"

"Sorry, Howard. He left at lunch for the golf course. I don't expect him back much before four o'clock. And knowing my husband, he may have a cocktail or two at the clubhouse after he takes his leisurely shower. Will you be staying at the office? I'll have him give you a call as soon as I see him."

"Yes. I'll go through some of my mail that has piled up over the last three days. I would appreciate hearing from Archibald. Thanks, Myra." His face spelled utter disappointment although he couldn't blame Archibald for being out on the course on such a beautiful day. If he hadn't been steeped so deeply into the Juliana Knecht investigation, he'd be out there himself. Even Ariel would have enjoyed hitting a few balls.

He replaced the phone in its cradle and walked over to Tony's desk. "Sorry Beardsley; no-go with Fortran right now. He's hitting a few balls on the course. If I were you, I'd get the heck out of this place and call Monica. More likely than not, we'll be on the hot seat until Monday morning. In a way, that's good. It will give both of us a chance to digest the events of the last three days. I'll take a look at the stuff sent to us from the Obispo Public Library, since Alice arranged the mail so carefully on my desk. I'll hang around until no later than five since Mrs. Fortran promised to have her husband call me when he gets home. If I have anything of importance, I'll call you later.

Go and take a rest. Thanks for all the driving—and a great job of record keeping."

"My pleasure, Chief. Don't get too caught up in those microfiche transmissions. See you Monday for sure." Howard watched his assistant hop on his motorbike and take off. He looked at the new mail more carefully and noticed that the envelopes were neatly arranged according to postmarks. He opened the first envelope mailed on Wednesday, September 25. Ms. Drew was true to her word.

Several articles had strictly to do with Horatio Alvis's run for the US Senate in 1964. Shepherd couldn't have cared less about that. It was water under the dam. He opened the second envelope.

Now this is more like it, thought he. The headline hit him right in the gut.

HORATIO ALVIS III CAUGHT IN FLAGRANTE DELICTO

Prominent member of the San Luis Obispo community presently in contention for a seat on the US Senate found in compromising scenario. Reporters for KEYX followed Alvis III on his campaign trail to the Morro Bay Yacht Club. He was observed having dinner at the club house with an unidentified young female. After a lengthy dinner showing Mr. Alvis in animated conversation with said female, the two were seen to board a yacht, the *Horatio III*, later identified as belonging to Mrs. Horatio Alvis III *née* Veronica Hofmeister, daughter of Governor and Senator Ludwig Hofmeister. Emerging from the yacht several hours later in a highly intoxicated state, Mr. Alvis's responses to the questioning reporter were clearly telling: "Get the f*** off my yacht; it's none of your damn business who I shag on my ship. You can quote me on your f*****g station or in your goddamn papers." Mr. Alvis ripped the camera from the reporter's hands and destroyed photographic evidence in his drunken stupor. He seated said unknown female in a waiting cab and then took off in his own Rolls-Royce.

Nice going Horatio! I knew you were a real bastard the moment I first laid eyes on you, mumbled Shepherd. He flipped through the other microfiche copies sent by Ms. Drew. There were several similar reportages, including those with embarrassing photographs taken of Mr. Alvis III and women other than his wife Veronica. Obviously, some reporters were more successful in their efforts of catching Horatio Alvis III in acts of sexual misconduct.

Commander Shepherd glanced at his wristwatch. It was ten minutes past five when his phone rang. He grabbed the receiver on the first ring: "Commander Shepherd, Precinct #18."

"Hi, Howard. It's Archibald. Sorry you caught me on the golf course when you returned. None of us had any idea you would be back on the weekend. Personally, I didn't expect to see you until sometime on Monday. Was it worth your while to make the trip up north?"

"Yes and no. Most of the interviews, perhaps better stated as interrogations, went pretty well. Some were more productive than others. One of the hardest things we had to do was to share the sad news with Juliana's mother. The harbormaster and commodore in Morro Bay provided helpful information as did our chat with young Horatio Alvis IV, a practicing physician in San Luis Obispo. The senior Alvis III and his wife were more challenging. I managed to collect some interesting evidence. However, I don't want to bother you on the weekend. Whatever I have can wait until Monday morning. To be honest, I need to get home to my Ariel, step back, and gain some distance between here and there. You know what I mean, don't you?"

"Yes, Howard. I could tell at the morgue how seeing the young victim and learning how she died and under what circumstance affected you. I'm sure you thought of your own beautiful daughter. You are a regular softy. Go home and enjoy being with your family. Juliana is perfectly safe and sound in my bailiwick. See you first thing Monday morning."

"Good point. Beardsley and I will see you at nine o'clock sharp on Monday. Have a great rest of the weekend." He replaced the receiver and removed the sealed envelope from his jacket's left breast pocket, placing it carefully into the safe behind his desk. He grabbed his hat and walked out to the car. He was laughing out loud as he approached his vehicle. Shepherd still couldn't fathom how he pulled off that trick with the Remington Rand.

Chapter 15

HOWARD Shepherd thoroughly enjoyed time spent with his wife Ariel and their daughter Claudia. He took a quick ride on his motorbike to the lighthouse after church on Sunday morning. He knew Homer and Sylvia would be interested to learn what discoveries he and Tony made up north. Homer and Sylvia had tears in their eyes as Howard shared with them the encounter with Juliana's mother. "We lost our son in Pearl Harbor; we can just imagine what that poor lady felt when you told her what happened to that beautiful young woman," voiced Sylvia. "So sad!" She kept dabbing her eyes with a lacy handkerchief as Homer caught her in a gentle embrace. "Keep us in the loop," said Homer as he walked Howard to his bike.

"I will, I will for sure. I know you truly care," and he stepped on the gas, anxious to get back to his loved ones. Monday morning couldn't come soon enough.

Homer looked admiringly at Sylvia. "That was very touching, speaking of Joshua as our son. I've told you before, you loved him from the moment you discovered that I fathered the boy. It didn't matter that Jenna had given him life. What

"

was important to you was that I had been given a son. When Joshua agreed to be adopted by us, you were as much of a mother to him as I was his father. He could never have been loved any more than he was loved by us. Thank you, Sylvia, for the woman you were and the loving wife you still are."

She reached out to him. "Thank you, Homer Elias, for speaking those kind words. I needed that just now." She did not attempt to hide her feelings.

⚹

Howard Shepherd, having parked his 1962 Plymouth in the parking lot, crossed paths with Tony Beardsley, whose only mode of transportation was his trusted Yamasaki motorbike. Monica was used to riding the back saddle unless, for dressy affairs, she had to engage Tony to be her chauffeur. "Glad you got my message. I didn't want to be late for our rendezvous at the mortuary. I need to stop by my desk and retrieve a certain letter—carefully." He winked at Tony, who couldn't help snickering. Tony laughed out loud when he saw Howard slip on gloves before retrieving the mysterious envelope from his safe. "I know it has some of my prints on the envelope; that couldn't be helped. But I don't want to muddy the waters any more than necessary. Let's go. I can't wait to hear Archibald's analysis."

They walked into Dr. Fortran's domain punctually at nine o'clock and were greeted with enthusiasm. "Might I ask what you are carrying so gingerly, never mind with gloved hands? Set it in that clean stainless steel pan, right over there—and tell me what it is all about."

"The last day in San Luis Obispo, we made our second call on

Alvis III and his wife. We were fortunate Veronica did not insist on having their attorney present. Actually, what happened was totally serendipitous and ultimately productive—I believe." Tony Beardsley had another snickering attack.

"What's so funny?" said the coroner.

"Wait until he tells you; I think it's hysterical."

"We were guided by their manservant, Ping, to Horatio Alvis III's office. As we walked in, the man had his back to us and I spotted this old, classic Remington Rand typewriter in the middle of his almost anally sterile desk. Unlike mine, you could've eaten off the damn thing. I don't know what made me do it, but it hit me like lightning as I shouted as if in shock about discovering that old thing. I went on and on about how thrilled I was to discover such a perfect antique machine and asked him if it was usable and in working order. I laid the schmaltz on so thick, Tony almost pissed in his pants. The dumb bastard fell for it."

"'Of course, it is in working order,' he yelled. He was totally flattered that some dumb cop could find it in his heart to appreciate his classic Remington sitting in a mansion otherwise dripping in modernity.

"With that he reached for a sheet of paper, inserted it, and asked if I remembered that silly sentence they made us type in school for practice purposes. 'You remember that old ditty, don't you?'"

"'The quick brown fox jumps over the lazy dog, said I."

"As quickly as I recited it, he typed away. I complimented him on his machine and his ability to use it so effectively, and then asked if he would mind letting me have the sheet as a souvenir to take home to Ariel, my wife, telling him what an avid admirer of such antiques she is. To make it even more convincing, I told him Ariel is a history buff and would eat up the whole thing. I yanked out my little Leica and took several photos of him and his trusted Remington Rand. He was most cooperative and responded positively to my request to fold the sheet neatly and insert it into a clean envelope. It was only after the quick brown fox was safely hidden in the breast pocket of my suit jacket that I came to more serious questions re his involvement in the case under investigation. Tony couldn't wait to get out of there. He was hardly able to take notes."

"That was pretty clever of you. I'm surprised he didn't catch on to what you were trying to do."

"I'm convinced it was the bravura and my totally out-of-character approach to my questions that threw him off guard. It was clearly evident in his facial expressions and his actions that he was overwhelmed by my 'sincere' flattery."

"Of course, I know where you are headed with this little act of deception," said Fortran. "Let me retrieve that pouch the young lady was carrying. Don't do anything with your mysterious envelope. Let me call in Morris Finkelstein, our fingerprint expert. I know he found some prints on that note in Juliana's pouch. I want him to handle the envelope and contents and see what he finds. Comparing the paper and the type on both pieces will be a cinch."

Morris Finkelstein appeared momentarily in Fortran's office. "Take a careful look at that envelope and its content. It's right over there in that clean bowl. There may be a few of Howard Shepherd's prints on the outside of the envelope; the inside ought to be pristine in terms of a certain individual's fingerprints. Take your time; we'll wait for your results." With that, Finkelstein disappeared to his lab—bowl and envelope in hand.

"So tell me, what else did you discover?" Tony recited details from the clipboard Howard had handed him before they left the Commander's office. Both he and Howard believed it was best not to miss any details.

"Sounds to me like you two had a couple very productive days. That meeting with the young woman's mother had to be a nail biter. I've always hated having to discuss death or the cause of death with loved ones. That's something they don't teach you in school. You learn it on the job—and some of us are better learners than others. I've never really become good at it. I'm glad it was you, Howard, who had to do it. I understand you've got the right touch."

"Finkelstein ought to have something for us real soon," Howard Shepherd spoke, while constantly tapping the desk with his pen. "Either he could read the damn prints or he couldn't. Of course, prints on some papers can be challenging since they tend to be thin and deteriorate rapidly. Well, let's hope for the best."

"Well, speak of the devil; no pun intended. What'ya got, doc?" said Tony Beardsley. Finkelstein's mien was noncommittal.

"The full sheet of paper has excellent prints that clearly originated with a singular individual. I compared these to some we lifted off that small note in the victim's pouch. They are a perfect match; there's absolutely no doubt, both pieces of paper were handled by one and the same person. Furthermore, both pieces were typed on the same typewriter and carry identical watermarks. There wasn't much of the watermark on the little note in the pouch, but enough to corroborate that they were from an identical source. I'll stop there," said Morris Finkelstein.

As out of one mouth: "Bingo," yelled the three onlookers. "You know your next move," said Fortran, addressing Commander Shepherd.

"I'm on it, Archibald," barked Shepherd as he was walking toward Alice Walker's desk.

"Get me the Chief of Police, San Luis Obispo, on the line, please. It's urgent. Thanks, Mrs. Walker." She knew he was hot under his collar. Rarely did he call her Mrs. Walker.

Chapter 16

ALICE Walker acted promptly; within seconds she had ascertained the direct line to the Chief of Police for the City of San Luis Obispo. She handed the note showing the number to the Commander, knowing that he sought to be the one making the first contact with his colleague. He bent toward his phone and dialed. The phone was picked up on the third ring.

"Carl Bronstein, Chief of Police, San Luis Obispo. How may I help you?"

"Commander Howard Shepherd, San Diego Police, precinct #18. We are investigating a possible murder in our jurisdiction which involves one of your citizens in San Luis Obispo. A colleague of mine and I did some investigation last Thursday and Friday. Evidence we obtained during our contacts clearly implicates Horatio Alvis III to be the subject in question. Fingerprints secured from Mr. Alvis III on Friday, September 27, 1968, match those found on a note uncovered on the victim when she was located last Tuesday morning on a stranded craft here in San Diego Bay. I'm asking you to arrest this man on suspicion of murder."

"You realize Mr. Horatio Alvis III and his wife are prominent citizens of this community?"

"I'm fully aware of it; however, the evidence is such that we have no other option but to assume that Mr. Alvis III is our person of interest."

"Wire me a copy of your detailed report; we will act according with your instructions. Thanks, Commander Shepherd. I'm sure we'll become better acquainted in the near future."

"I'm certain we will. Thanks, Chief Bronstein," and the connection was gone.

⋈

On the afternoon of October 4, 1968, to be exact, at one o'clock, a police cruiser pulled up in front of the Alvis mansion. One of the three police officers jumped from the car and pressed the doorbell firmly. Ping responded promptly.

"Who's carring, prease?"

"Open this gate at once. It's San Luis Obispo police."

The wrought iron gate began moving immediately. As soon as the cruiser had reached the front of the mansion, the three cops stormed up the ornate stairway leading to the entry. Ping barely got out of the way, fearing he'd be knocked down. Veronica, having overheard the brief conversation on the intercom system, entered the room in her inimitable style and grace.

"How may I be of assistance to you, gentlemen?" She let her words hang in midair, looking the men up and down in her well-known arrogant manner.

"We are here to arrest your husband, Horatio Alvis III, on suspicion of murder. Please lead us to him at once." Veronica remained absolutely cool; it was almost as if she had expected to hear those words just spoken.

"Ping, show these men to my husband's office." Ping walked the men toward the back of the house, hesitatingly pointing to the door in question. "That mastel's office." He let them pass.

Hartwick Mason, the oldest of the three cops, pushed the door open without having knocked. Horatio, totally surprised, stared at the three cops standing before him. "Horatio Alvis III we are arresting you on suspicion of murder of a Juliana A. D. Knecht. You have the right to remain silent. Anything you say can and will be used against you in a court of law. You have the right to an attorney. If you cannot afford an attorney, one will be provided for you. Do you understand the rights I have just read to you? With these rights in mind, do you wish to speak to me?"

Horatio was still staring at Officer Hartwick Mason, not fully comprehending his words although he knew instantly what they meant. He yelled for Veronica.

"Get on the phone and call Max Weinstein. Have Max meet me at the police station where these men are taking me." He didn't say another word.

"Where are you taking my husband?"

"He'll be processed at Police Headquarters on 4300 Samson Boulevard in downtown San Luis Obispo." Officer Hartwick walked around Horatio's desk, putting handcuffs on him. "Since you are fully dressed, there's no need for further delay. If you need to use a restroom, I shall accompany you."

Horatio nodded affirmatively and moved toward a small WC conveniently located off his office quarters. Hartwick assisted Horatio with the unzipping of his fly. "I believe there is enough play in those cuffs. For the rest, you're on your own." He stepped back, letting Horatio take care of business. Horatio flushed and turned to wash his hands over the elaborate sink. "Hope you don't mind if I do the same?" Horatio gave him a nod, just waiting to be taken away. *Don't know how all of this shall end,* his mind said as he was replaying scenes that took place during the past week.

Veronica watched as they guided Horatio out of their mansion. Neither said a word. A sardonic smile entered her tight face as she saw Horatio being pushed into the backseat of the police cruiser. She turned away, headed for the closest telephone, and dialed Max Weinstein's number.

"Max, Horatio has just been arrested by the police. They did their Miranda thing and have taken him to Police Headquarters. I don't have to tell you where it is. He's asked me to speak with you and have you meet him at the station. He hasn't breathed a word."

"I'll be on my way down there shortly," replied Max.

She checked her hair and makeup in the front-hall mirror. The seams of her stockings were straight. Glancing at her elegant black dress, she approved of her appearance. "Ping, bring the Rolls-Royce around. You'll have to play chauffeur for a change. I'm not in the mood for searching out convenient parking near Police Headquarters."

Veronica pulled the front door shut and walked down toward Ping who was holding the right rear door open for her. He closed the door gently and headed for the driver's seat.

Ping loved the few occasions when he was out in public and especially when he was allowed to drive the black Rolls-Royce. Of course, he had to adjust the seat to accommodate his slight stature.

"Keep driving as if we were going to the Friday markets. Once we'll get into the city, I'll direct you to Police Headquarters on Samson Blvd.," said she.

"Yes, Ma'am" was all Ping answered and drove, always looking straight ahead. He was hoping other manservants in the neighborhood would spot him driving his master's fancy rig.

Chapter 17

MAX Weinstein arrived shortly after they booked Horatio. He was facing the interrogating officer, Commander Fred Lloyd, in a brightly lit examining room. Max was seated next to Horatio. Holding up one of the photographs taken at the morgue in San Diego, Commander Lloyd fired his first question:

"Are you familiar with this person?" Max looked at Horatio and realized that he knew who she was. "You may answer that question."

"Yes. She was an acquaintance of our son, Horatio Alvis IV."

"When did you see her last, if you recall?" Weinstein raised an eyebrow.

"I believe I saw her shortly after the first of the year, perhaps even late last year. I'm not sure any longer."

"Let me remind you, anything you say can and will be used against you in a court of law. Do you recognize the copies of these papers I am presenting to you? The originals are held at the coroner's office in San Diego. These represent evidence on the basis of which we have arrested you."

Both Horatio and Weinstein glared at the messages. "My client refuses to answer the question."

"These papers were typed on the Remington Rand typewriter that was found to exist in your offices in your home. Both pieces clearly bear your fingerprints and attest incontrovertibly to the fact that you were the author of both documents."

"My client has nothing more to say. I consider this interrogation over. We'll see you in court." Horatio was taken to a cell. Max Weinstein was looking around for Veronica Alvis as soon as he left the examining room.

X

Bail was set at one million dollars, which was met by Veronica Alvis. Ping caught the three of them as they emerged from a side door of the courthouse, attempting to avoid being spotted by reporters on duty representing the local media. Max was the first to speak; Veronica and Horatio were still in shock.

"As soon as we get to the house, I want us to confer in private in your office. You may want to consider giving Ping the afternoon off."

"That's an excellent idea," agreed Veronica.

"Ping, go for a bike ride after lunch. It's such a nice, sunny fall day. You may want to call your buddy and have him join you for the outing." She reached into her purse and pulled out a twenty-dollar bill, passing it to Horatio riding in the front passenger seat. "Here, press this into Ping's hand. I want him to enjoy the afternoon."

Ping fixed a very light lunch for the Alvis's and their attorney. "Just take the plates and napkins to my husband's office, Ping. All of us have what we wish to drink. Hope you'll enjoy your outing." She smiled at him in an insincere manner; Ping reciprocated in typical Asian mode.

Veronica followed Ping out the door and made sure the gate was closed after their manservant had passed it on his bike. Ping knew the code for activating the gate, which he would utilize upon his eventual return before dusk.

She faced Horatio and Max as she closed the office door softly behind her. Max fired the opening salvo.

"Would you mind telling me how they got ahold of that incriminating evidence obviously produced on this Remington typewriter? And don't tell me you had nothing to do with either of those documents. Remember, I'm your attorney and am supposed to help you—not fight you. I certainly don't want to have to deal with any surprises in a courtroom."

"I have no idea who wrote the note they found on that woman washed ashore in San Diego. I shouldn't say 'that woman.' I do know who she is and the name under which she was introduced to me. I did type that crazy sentence on the Remington when those guys from San Diego were speaking to me on Friday last week. I don't know what possessed me to do it, but the Commander was so taken by that old and still-functioning machine that I acted upon his requests. I suppose that was a mistake. Would you say that he tricked me into doing it?"

"That wouldn't wash in court; the cat's out of the bag. I still don't know how they can claim that fingerprints on both pieces match yours. Are you sure you are telling me everything? You cannot hide such things from me. It will really backfire if they come up with other evidence that links you to the contents of that mystery pouch on this woman, Juliana A. D. Knecht. What do you know about her? How do you know her?"

"As I mentioned on several occasions, our son introduced her to me. She was a casual acquaintance of his. Apparently, they met in medical school pursuing different disciplines. He had dinner with her a few times and took her out on that old boat we had given to him as a present. From what he told me, she liked the little craft and was somehow taken by the name *Arabella*. She loved being out on the water and wanted to learn more about sailing." He could feel Veronica's eyes boring through him. He hadn't succeeded in hiding his lying from her.

"Alright, alright! I fucked her a couple of times earlier this year. She told me she was on the pill and didn't want me to wear any condoms. Big mistake. I'm sure I wasn't the father of the kid she was carrying. According to what I remember, she would've been much closer to delivery than what the coroner estimated her to be when she washed ashore. It can't be me who got her knocked up. Besides, closer to the timeline in question, I'd dropped her like a hot potato; I was fooling around with a more mature blond and a red-haired hooker. They were a lot safer."

"You bastard," screamed Veronica. "No wonder the press had a field day with your peccadilloes and made it impossible for you to join the ranks of honorable men in Washington, honorable men like my father." Veronica knew instantly she had overstepped the bounds of believability.

"Bullshit, bullshit! Honorable men! Your father was as crooked as they come. How the hell did you think he got as rich as he was? He knew the system, and the old buzzard knew how to milk it to kingdom come. When it came to women, he was just

smarter than I; he didn't get caught getting laid by anything he could put his hands on—most of the time. I remember your mother. You are a chip right off the old ice block."

Veronica spit in his face and walked out of the room.

Max intervened. "This isn't getting us anywhere, Horatio. We've got important other matters to discuss. Judge Horace Blunder is assigned to your case. He's inclined to go along with the change of venue sought by the San Diego authorities. They want you transported to San Diego and tried in a San Diego court. Personally, I'm in support of the idea and wouldn't fight it. You might deal with a less biased jury. Unlike here, most people in San Diego have never heard of you or Veronica's family."

"I suppose you have a good point. Will that mean that I will be sitting in some jail cell in San Diego?"

"No, no. Your bail will still apply in a different county; you will simply have to make it known exactly where you will reside during the trial. For now, Veronica's largesse of affording you one million dollars in bail will protect you. As it stands, I better get busy and check out anything that I can lay my hands on before we go to trial. I presume that Veronica is aware of the possible costs that will be associated with your defense?"

"I have no doubt she's fully apprised of it." He poured two healthy snifters of Glenlivet, knowing it was Max's preferred drink.

"Here's to your success in getting me out of this mess!" Horatio lifted his glass toward Max and then held it up to the light pouring in through the large picture window. Admiringly, he approved of the brilliant color of their libation.

Chapter 18

THE phone rang at the Alvis mansion. These days, Veronica or Horatio would reach immediately for a receiver, never giving Ping a chance to answer.

"Alvis's."

"Good morning, Veronica. It's Max calling. I've heard from San Diego. Judge Nathaniel Horowitz has been assigned to Horatio's case. A tentative trial date has been set for January 1969. Jury selection may commence early in the month. I'm hoping to get the prospective witness list from the prosecutor's offices. That's all I have for you at this time.

"Thought it would be helpful for you to know where things stand at the moment as we are approaching the holiday season. I'm glad our high holy days are behind us. We had a meaningful service for Yom Kippur at our temple on October 2. I don't attend regularly, but Miriam insists I make an effort on Yom Kippur. Please let me know if Horatio or you have any questions and concerns. I have a busy court schedule coming up; if you don't reach me right away, leave me a message on my recorder."

"Thanks, Max, for letting us know. I'll tell Horatio you called. He must be in the shower since he didn't pick up his phone. These days he seems to be always sitting on a hot seat. Speaking of Yom Kippur, I have to check out the family's gravesite before November 1. We have a great service looking after my parents' final resting place, but now and then these folks seem to forget certain important days. I want to make sure the candles are in place and lit for the occasion. My mother always made a point of it when she was tending the graves of my grandparents. Of course, Horatio's parents are buried close to the Oregon border. We don't make it up there very often."

"Speaking of gravesites, I learned that Coroner Fortran released the body of Juliana A. D. Knecht to her mother. Juliana was buried in a very private ceremony at Forest Lawn in Glendale where her father, Anton Knecht, was interred many years ago. Apparently, Mrs. Knecht chose not even to have an obituary in any papers. Under the circumstances, I can't really blame the poor woman."

"To tell you the God's honest truth, I know very little about her. I cannot imagine how I would handle Junior's death were I confronted with such a situation. He's in his thirties but still my one and only baby. He hates it when I call him that. It's a mother's thing. I wasn't always the best of mothers when he was very young; but once he started walking and talking, he couldn't do any wrong. I couldn't have any more children and am honest enough to say, I spoiled the dickens out of him. He was and is the smartest and best son any mother could have."

"You realize he will be called as a witness, don't you? If for no other reason than that he knew Juliana A. D. Knecht and introduced her to his father. I still can't believe what your husband owned up to just days ago. Give me a break. How horny could he have been? Carrying on a sexual relationship with his son's former girlfriend? I guess we can't even call her that; she was a close acquaintance of your son's, if there is such a thing." He kept shaking his head in total disbelief. In his lengthy marriage, he had had a few trysts along the way, but nothing comparable to what his client had succeeded in doing.

"You really don't want me to comment on what you just shared with me? I just hope Junior's name will not be dragged through his father's mud. I would not want him to be personally and professionally harmed by his father's unseemly behavior. That's all I can pray for, not that I'm a praying woman. I can't wait for this trial to start and to get it over with, no matter what the outcome. If Horatio indeed had a hand in this woman's death, I hope they throw the book at him. He's to be pitied. I rue the day I first laid eyes on him thirty-six years ago."

"Why did you marry him? You came from such totally different backgrounds?"

"That was just it. I saw in Horatio someone who would allow me to escape the world in which I grew up. His father was a respected man in academia and in the community. I saw a nice guy in Horatio. He was obviously taken by my good looks and my hefty pocketbook. People living on the outside assumed that my world was prestige, glamor, and wealth. For most of my life, I didn't even want to talk about my upbringing. There were times when I considered counseling and analysis.

"Most of my friends and acquaintances had no idea what a miserable bastard my father was. When we lived in DC, where I grew up, he chased every skirt and screwed everything he could put his hands on. In the early days, we lived in elegant hotels, Father having his trysts in some other lodging, perhaps even some whorehouses. Things turned for the worse when Senator Hofmeister decided to buy a suburban villa. Eventually, he thought nothing of bringing his paramours home. Mother and I had to listen to the shenanigans going on under our own roof. On a few occasions, he was apparently so desperate for sex he threatened to rape me. That was where my mother drew the line."

Max kept looking at his watch. "Can we talk about this some other time? I'm absolutely blown away by what you are telling me."

"Give me just a couple more minutes. I don't often open up to anyone about this. Since you asked, let me finish, please.

"My mother made every possible effort to protect him and to hide his philandering; God help him, had he laid a hand on me. Father ruled the roost with an iron fist and often used that iron fist to abuse my mother. I don't remember how often I saw her bruised all over and crying quietly in her bedroom. My mother was not a cold person; but after years of physical, mental, and psychological abuse, she withdrew into her own world.

"Things got even worse when we moved into the governor's mansion in Sacramento in 1930. When I met Horatio in 1932 on a blind date, I was full of hope, wanting to get away from the nightmares I experienced in that old burg on "H" Street. Mother was thrilled when Dad was defeated running for his second term. During his reelection campaign, the Paparazzi caught him red-handed with a hooker in some fleabag motel in San Francisco. It was all over the papers in the biggest headlines you can imagine. Two weeks later, he dropped dead with a massive heart attack.

"Horatio must have been taken in by my father's amorous adventures, wanting to emulate that dark side of the 'respectable' man. We left Sacramento and moved into a nice place in San Luis Obispo. When my mother died in 1936, Horatio and I moved into our present home. It had belonged to my maternal grandparents for many years. Since Mother was an only child, I inherited the place. In time, Horatio and I completely renovated and updated the familial mansion to our liking.

"So, you see, that was the model I was exposed to. I suppose, I'm to blame. I introduced Horatio to my world. Coming from his sedate background, he might have been intrigued by my father's dark sides, wanting to explore avenues he never walked. He must have seen it as more fun screwing around rather than being the faithful husband I sought and wanted.

"Often, I tried buying his love with my money; the way things turned out, I was obviously even a failure in doing that. Being totally disenchanted with marital bliss, I began to hate all men. I withdrew from our marital bed and let Horatio seek his pleasures wherever he chose. I didn't care that he dubbed me his rich-bitch ice block. All I cared about was raising our son to be a decent human being. Utterly disappointed in my life, I try hiding behind my glamorous facade, drowning myself many a night in an abundance of alcohol. That's how you have gotten to know me."

Max took an audibly deep breath. "I'm so sorry to learn all this, Veronica. I had no idea what you experienced in your home during your formative years. Knowing what your father really was like, and how he treated your mother, certainly would shape and impact your own life. Hearing what you just told me makes me look at you and Horatio with different eyes; you've conveyed another image than the one in my mind. Believe me,

I feel for you." She could tell by his breathing pattern that he was anxious to get off the phone. It pleased her to have disclosed to Max what bothered her so intensely.

Max finally found his voice. "I hate to cut you short. The burdens of the trial are summoning me. Glad we had this chance to talk, Veronica. Fill Horatio in on what I reported to you. I've got to get going. My desk is piled high with briefs. It's good to be popular, but this is getting almost too much. Sayonara. We'll talk again real soon." He hung up before Veronica could say one more word.

Veronica was relieved she didn't have to say another word. Completely out of character, she was stifling her sobs into a handkerchief. She didn't want Ping or anyone else to hear her cries for help.

Chapter 19

ARABELLA Knecht was in Glendale, visiting with the stone-mason who had designed and executed the black granite marker she had chosen when Anton passed away suddenly in 1946. Juliana was barely twelve years old. She looked up at the man, tears streaming down her face.

"Who would have thought you would be adding our daughter's name to the stone before completing mine? I always knew I wanted to be buried next to my dear husband. That's why I had you add my name to his already, twenty-one years ago; that is, all but for the date of my final departure. Where did those years go?

"I loved Anton and miss him terribly. Juliana was my everything after being widowed at such a young age. I was only thirty-five when Anton died. I was always thankful that he left us well-off financially and I didn't have to worry about how to raise and educate my girl. Anton had established trusts for both of us that were envisioned to take care of us for the rest of our days. You are probably too busy to listen to the outpourings of this old woman, right?"

"No, not at all, Mrs. Knecht. It is such a sad story. I wish things had turned out differently for you and your dear daughter. Sometimes we need to find a caring soul, willing to listen to what concerns us the most at the moment. I'm not that busy. Don't stop sharing your story with me."

"When Juliana went off to college in 1952, I was awfully lonely in our big house. You know what it was like? I had help in the house and landscapers and a pool man who took care of the outside. And yet, I was so lonesome and sad. Friends encouraged me to get married again, but I never met another man I could love the way I loved Anton.

"But—things do have a way of working out. Two years later my mother died and left me their darling little house in San Luis Obispo. I was able to sell the house in Glendale and made mother's house my own. I redesigned the gardens and completely redid the inside of the house to my own tastes. Kitchen and baths were very much in need of updating. Of course, all of that was easily possible due to my financial security. While I didn't have the happiest memories looking back at my upbringing in San Luis Obispo, I learned to love the little house, and even more so, making new friends with my neighbors. Juliana enjoyed coming home and spent holidays and breaks from school with me. We made a great mother-daughter duo. And now, she's gone. I still cannot believe what happened." She bent her head and sobbed uncontrollably.

Stonemason Heraldo Herbert rose from his chair and gave Mrs. Knecht a reassuring hug. "There, there. You cry all you need to. Let it all out. In my profession, I've learned that crying is good for our souls."

"You are a good man, Mr. Herbert. I remember how you consoled me after Anton's untimely passing. I still like the plot I chose at the time. I've spoken to the caretaker. After the ground has settled in a few weeks, he will completely redo the layout. One thing I asked him to plant this fall in profusion is deep purple Superstition Bearded Iris; they were always Juliana's favorite spring flowers. You may want to consider adding Juliana's name to the stone before all this other work is done. I want her name to be shown as Juliana Arabella Davos Knecht 1934-1968. To be quite honest with you, I still do not know the day she actually died. Perhaps the inquest and trial may be conclusive."

Mr. Herbert's arms enfolded Arabella once again. "Be assured everything will be done to your satisfaction. I know the gardener very well; he's top notch. You don't have to worry about a thing. After I engrave the stone, I'll give it a thorough cleaning. It hasn't been done for a few years. These things happen when we live far apart. I could put it on my calendar and automatically do it every other year. It's not that costly."

"Not to worry about costly, I would appreciate your looking after the grave. Just put the bill in the mail, and you know I'm good for the money. After Juliana's death, I've given much thought to creating an endowment with Forest Lawn, allowing for care in perpetuity after I'm gone. Guess that's for another day." She shook hands with Mr. Herbert and turned away. She did not want to upset the caring man with another flood of her tears.

Chapter 20

MAX volunteered to drive the Rolls-Royce to San Diego. It made for a comfortable ride for all three of them. He arranged for hotel lodgings near Union Street, in walking distance from the courthouse. Veronica advised him not to spare any expense. If nothing else, she wanted to come back to comfortable accommodations after trying days at court.

Jury selection had started January 6. Both prosecutor, Hermione Grand, and defense attorney, Max Weinstein, were judicious during the process. More than sixty individuals had been summoned for jury duty. A group of twelve was seated in the jury box, having been drawn from the jury pool. Questioned in turn by Ms. Grand, Mr. Weinstein, and on occasion by Judge Horowitz, jurors were selected or rejected by the respective parties based on the responses given.

Nine men and three women were ultimately chosen for the final twelve by Friday, January 10, with the trial set to commence on Monday, January 13, 1969. Judge Horowitz swore in the jury with each respective juror taking the oath: "I solemnly and sincerely declare and affirm that I will give a true verdict according to the evidence," they spoke en masse. The jurors were dismissed by the judge with appropriate admonitions and were allowed to leave the courtroom as soon as Judge Horowitz had vacated the bench.

"I'm glad that's over," said Veronica. "I'm not sure about the choice of two of the women jurors. They struck me as predisposed. Of course, you and Ms. Grand wouldn't want *me* to serve on that jury, speaking of predisposed!" She forced her eyes to take in the ceiling of the hotel lobby.

"What I need is a stiff drink. I don't know about you gentlemen, but I'm heading for the nearest watering hole." With that, Veronica Alvis crossed the highly polished marble floor, her high heels clicking noisily, much to the annoyance of men quietly trying to converse, as she made her way to the bar. She hiked onto the first barstool she detected, getting the attention of the busy bartender. "Pour me a triple Remy Martin. Skip the ice. I want it as straight as possible." The handsome dog behind the bar got her drift.

"Tough day at court? Ha? Here you are, Ma'am. Enjoy. I don't get too many orders for triples; that's telling."

Horatio and Max finally arrived and were lucky two gentlemen had just vacated two seats next to Veronica. "Good timing, boys, these seats are preheated. Rest your arses and order whatever tickles your fancy" were Veronica's words—becoming slightly slurred. Max became alarmed when she drew circles above her snifter, conveying to the bartender to hit her again.

"You better go easy on that stuff. Neither Horatio nor I are in shape to carry you to your bed."

"That'a be a new one, me being carried by my husband to bed. He's much better at that with bimbos. I'm too heavy for him."

Max grabbed her by the arm, holding her glass. "Veronica, don't embarrass yourself. I know you are out of town, but someone will surely recognize you. Remember, you are still a lady. Don't finish that second drink. There's a nice restaurant in the hotel. You need a decent meal; that's your problem." He encouraged her to get off the barstool and was glad he held onto her. She would have hit that unforgiving marble floor full force. No matter how hard he tried, she would not relinquish her drink. Both he and Horatio held her firmly and guided Veronica safely to a seat in the dining room. The wait staff were making eyes and obviously wondering with whom they were dealing.

Menus were presented promptly and glasses of lemon water served immediately. "Would you like me to order you an Espresso?" said Horatio.

"Why? And get rid of this wonderful buzz? I don't want to be sober tonight. I couldn't face my bed and the night thinking about the reality of this Pandora's box about to be opened. Max talks about I embarrassing myself. He has no clue how you will embarrass me by the time this damn trial is over. He doesn't know the half of what's coming down the pike. If I were near the bar, I'd order another drink from that gorgeous hunk behind the counter. I don't want any food. Just get me the hell out of this place."

Veronica tried to stand up and was inwardly glad for her male companions who caught her. Max and Horatio excused themselves, letting the waitstaff know they would be back shortly. They got her on the elevator and to their room. Horatio attempted to undress his wife, and finally just tucked her in under the down comforter, clothes and all. He had no difficulty freeing her of her high heels. She passed out without uttering another word. Leaving Veronica in the arms of Morpheus, Horatio and Max closed the hotel room door quietly, heading back to the dining room and a much-needed decent meal.

No one inquired as to the state of the lady. Meals ordered were served in hushed voices. There weren't many hotel guests in the restaurant on this Friday night. "Looks like my dear wife scared away the few guests who were in the dining room when we dragged her out of here. I hope no one recognized her," said Horatio.

"I believe she is truly worried about the trial. As unforgiving as she is toward you—and perhaps rightfully so—she seems to be even more concerned about your son and herself. She's particularly worried about the impact this trial may have on her social standing and reputation and that of her family. I must assume that you have been forthright with me; what I'm not looking for are surprises from testimony by any witnesses called by the prosecution. Let's hope Veronica's fears are unfounded," were Max's observations. The two men shook hands before they entered their respective hotel rooms.

Chapter 21

WALKING into the courthouse, Veronica admired the beauty of the neoclassic style of the architecture. The building was spotless, the woodwork gleaming, and the chandeliers shining brightly, casting long shadows as the three figures moved slowly down the hallways to the designated courtroom. Finally, Max Weinstein spoke.

"After the jury is seated and Judge Horowitz has given his initial instructions, Ms. Grand will make her opening statement, followed by mine. Looking over the list of witnesses the prosecution is calling, Homer Annapolis will be first. Perhaps you don't remember, he is the lighthouse tour guide who first reported the stranded cutter on the shore. Just sit quietly and listen and be prepared for long sessions of testimony.

"Veronica, you will be seated in the row directly behind us. I know it's not easy for you, but please refrain from making any comments—might they be appropriate or inappropriate—and do not let any challenging situations be reflected in your mien. While no courtroom photography will be allowed, the presence of a courtroom artist has been sanctioned, permitting that person to sketch anyone present during all aspects of the trial. These sketches are subject to release to the media. So, please be on your guard."

The number of spectators turned out to be greater than expected. Brief mention of the upcoming trial of Horatio Alvis III had been made on the evening news on KNSD. Max Weinstein looked over his right shoulder. He saw Commander Shepherd and Sergeant Beardsley speaking quietly to an elderly gentleman. He didn't know who Homer Annapolis was. He surmised that the other man seated near the police officers was perhaps Coroner Fortran, whose name was shown on the witness list for the prosecution.

The door to the judges' chambers opened. Robed in traditional black, Judge Nathaniel Horowitz approached the bench. Bailiff Brad Butler sprang into action.

"Please rise. The Court of the Ninth Judicial Circuit, Criminal Division, is now in session, the Honorable Judge Nathaniel Horowitz presiding." Judge Horowitz addressed the Court:

"Everyone but the jury may be seated. Mr. Butler, please swear in the jury." Bailiff Butler faced the jury.

"Please raise your right hand. Do you solemnly swear or affirm that you will truly listen to this case and render a true verdict and a fair sentence as to this defendant?" The jurors spoke en masse:

"I do."

"You may be seated," declared Bailiff Butler.

As soon as the jury had taken their relatively comfortable seats, Judge Horowitz addressed the jury.

"Members of the jury, your duty today will be to determine whether the defendant is guilty or not guilty based only on facts and evidence provided in this case. The prosecution has the burden of proving the guilt of the defendant beyond a reasonable doubt. This burden remains on the prosecution through the trial. The prosecution must prove that a crime was committed and that the defendant is the person who committed the crime. However, if you are not satisfied of the defendant's guilt to that extent, then reasonable doubt exists and the defendant must be found not guilty. Mr. Butler, what is today's case?"

"Your Honor, today's case is The State of California versus Horace Alvis III."

Judge Horowitz faced Hermione Grand: "Is the prosecution ready?"

Ms. Grand stood up: "Yes, Your Honor," and was instructed by the judge to be seated.

Likewise, the judge addressed Max Weinstein. "Is the defense ready?"

Max Weinstein rose from his seat: "Yes, Your Honor," and was given permission to take his seat.

Hermione Grand stood up and stepped in front of the jury box. Her vision swept across the faces of the twelve jurors, making eye contact, however fleetingly, with each and every one of the twelve who held the fate of the defendant in their hands. She turned to face Judge Horowitz.

"Your Honor, members of the Jury, my name is Hermione Grand, representing the State of California in this case."

Large images of Juliana A. D. Knecht taken at the mortuary were projected on a sizable screen located to the left of the judge's bench; the final image being the enlarged photo taken from Juliana's California driver's license. Lighting conditions were such that the images shown could be viewed most positively.

"The images before your eyes are those of Juliana A. D. Knecht, who we believe was murdered by the defendant Horatio Alvis III of San Luis Obispo. We intend to prove beyond reasonable doubt that Mr. Alvis III was indeed the individual responsible for the death of this vital young woman and her unborn child. Please find the defendant guilty after weighing all evidence presented in this court of law. Thank you."

A hush had fallen over the courtroom. No one had expected the prosecution's opening statement to be of such brevity. Nevertheless, the concise statement paired with the powerful images transcended to the jury and all others present. Those who were privy to do so watched the courtroom artist furiously attempting to capture the facial expressions of the prosecutor as she presented her case.

Judge Horowitz addressed Hermione Grand. "Prosecution, you may call your first witness."

"Thank you, your Honor. I call to the stand Homer Annapolis."

Homer Annapolis approached the front of the courtroom.

"Will the witness please remain standing to be sworn in by the bailiff?"

Bailiff Butler looked at Homer Annapolis. "Please raise your right hand. Do you swear to tell the truth, the whole truth, and nothing but the truth?" Homer's blood chilled as he touched the Bible held out to him by Bailiff Butler.

"I do," said Homer, who then walked to the witness stand and sat down.

Hermione Grand was a firm believer in making eye

contact with any person with whom she wished to engage in a conversation. It made no difference that the person was a witness, a judge, a professional colleague or adversary, friend or foe. Her vision was never directed toward a floor or a ceiling. Thus she approached Homer Annapolis.

"Please state your full name." Grand's eyes met Homer's straight on.

"My name is Homer Elias Annapolis."

"I understand you are the lighthouse keeper at Point Loma, is this correct?"

"No Ma'am. The old lighthouse has not had a keeper since 1891. I was a lighthouse keeper at Point Arena for many years until I retired from active duty in 1963. At that time, my wife, Sylvia, and I became volunteers for the National Park Services and serve as reenactors at the old Point Loma lighthouse. It is in that capacity I functioned on September 24, 1968, when I discovered a stranded boat on the shores of the Cabrillo National Monument."

Color slides taken by Commander Howard Shepherd were projected for the benefit of the jury.

"Please tell us something about these slides."

"After the terrible western storm that struck most of the California coast on Sunday, September 22, we were completely shrouded in thick fog. When the fog finally began to lift, I spotted a stranded boat through my looking glass. As difficult as it is these days for me to manage such a steep incline toward the shore, I overcame my trepidations and made it to the site of the boat."

"Why did the hike down to the shore appear to be difficult for you? You seem to be a man in excellent physical condition."

"Madam Prosecutor, in this case, looks are deceiving. I am eighty-five years old. True, I'm well conditioned and my life was always linked to the sea and hard physical work. That's what made me stay in shape. I became one of four lighthouse keepers at Point Arena in 1904 for the first time. The lighthouse went down with the 1906 earthquake. I was reassigned when the lighthouse was rebuilt in 1908. My wife and I lived for the next fifty-five years as keepers of the lighthouse until we retired in 1963. It was there that we raised our son, our only child, who was killed at Pearl Harbor." Hermione Grand's face registered sadness and compassion for the handsome old man on the witness stand.

"I'm so sorry to learn of your tragic loss. But now, tell us something about the conditions of the vessel as you found it."

"As you can see in that first slide, both masts of the craft were shattered by wind and sea. All of the rigging was ripped away by the storm. It's a miracle that this boat did not sink."

"I understand you were the first person to get on the deck of the stranded vessel. How did you manage to do that, and what did you discover?"

"With stranded materials I created a rather primitive plank allowing me to climb aboard the boat. There was some seawater in depressions of the deck, but not enough to sink her. Near the bow I spotted a bunch of seaweed. The craft must have been dragged through the kelp forest close to the shoreline. I ventured into the hull and discovered a lot of broken glass and pottery. Further investigation led me to the discovery of a human body just beyond a heavy fabric curtain next to the bulkhead. The nature of the hull on a cutter is such that the average male cannot stand up straight. Furthermore, I failed to carry a flashlight with me. With the limited light available within the hull, I saw the body but could not discern whether it was male or female."

"What did you do next?"

"I made it back up the hill as quickly as possible, alerted my wife Sylvia to what I saw, and then rode my bike to the nearest police station, which is Precinct #18. I related my findings to Commander Howard Shepherd of the San Diego PD, who took over at this point."

"You have anything to add to your statements?"

"No. I believe I have stated all that is pertinent to my observations."

Judge Horowitz cleared his throat: "The defense may cross-examine the witness."

"Defense has no questions for the witness. Thank you, your Honor," said Max Weinstein.

"You may step down," said Judge Horowitz to the witness. Homer walked to the back of the courtroom. *They took the wind out of your sails*, Sylvia thought.

"Prosecution, you may call your next witness."

"Thank you, your Honor. I call to the stand Commander Howard Shepherd."

Commander Shepherd walked to the front of the courtroom.

"Will the witness please remain standing to be sworn in by the bailiff?"

Bailiff Butler addressed Commander Shepherd. "Please raise your right hand. Do you swear to tell the truth, the whole truth, and nothing but the truth?" Commander Howard Shepherd placed his right hand firmly on the Bible held in front of him.

"I do," said Commander Shepherd, who then walked to the witness stand and sat down.

At this very moment the door to the courtroom was held by a young clerk, admitting a tiny lady fully dressed in black. Her hair was concealed by a black cloche; a serious veil disguised her face. She seated herself in the back row of the courtroom. The mysterious lady merely nodded toward the helpful young man in recognition of his courtesies.

Hermione Grand approached the witness.

"Please state your full name." Her eyes appeared to be boring through the man; she had his full attention.

"My name is Howard Jerome Shepherd, Commander and Chief, San Diego PD, Precinct #18."

"Please state how you were involved with the case of the present defendant."

"Three of my staff and myself were alerted to a stranded boat by Mr. Homer Annapolis, who presently volunteers at the Old Point Loma Lighthouse. The man was clearly shook when he discovered a body on the floor of the hull of the vessel precariously settled on the shores near Cabrillo National Monument."

"What specifically did you see when you arrived on the scene?"

"Our first impression of the boat was such that we wondered how it could have survived the storm and landed on our shores. We created access to the deck by using two solid planks that we carried on our transport. The makeshift gangway created by Mr. Annapolis would never have allowed any of my men or myself to gain access to the deck safely. Officer Beardsley and I inspected the body described to be lying in the back portion of the hull by Homer Annapolis."

"Please describe in detail how the body was positioned."

"Using a powerful flashlight, we ascertained first of all that the body in question was female. The scene within the chamber was such that Mr. Annapolis had not been able to determine the sex of the body in the absence of a good light source. The woman was lying only slightly on her back and favored the right side. I touched her neck with my gloved hand only to discover that the woman was indeed dead. Unquestionably, she had been dead for hours. There was no evidence of any kind of struggle. She appeared to be quite peaceful although her right hand was firmly clutched. In the presence of rigor mortis, we could not determine if she merely closed her hand tightly or if she was holding onto an object. Her eyes were closed and she appeared to be just sound asleep and at rest."

Faint sounds of crying were heard from the back row of the courtroom. The woman in black was clearly touched by the testimony of Commander Shepherd. Judge Horowitz elected not to act upon the mild auditory disruption. He disliked intensely when undesirable sounds interfered with the procedures of a trial.

"Please continue with your testimony, Commander," said Ms. Grand.

"A second of my officers on the scene, Sergeant Harry Townsend, I designated to record any observations Sergeant Beardsley and I were making. Sergeant Townsend is too big a guy to function in the confining space of that cutter. Having brought a stretcher onboard deck, Sergeant Beardsley and I lifted the woman's body carefully off the floor of the hull with the intent of taking her eventually up the hill and to our paddy wagon. It was only when we lifted her body that we discovered a small pouch suspended from the waist of the young woman.

Although gloved at all times, I elected not to examine the contents of said pouch, preferring that it be inspected by the coroner, Dr. Fortran. We made sure the body of the woman was covered with a clean sheet preventing contact with any investigatory insects."

Hermione Grand smiled at the last comment made by Commander Shepherd. "That was very considerate of you. Now tell us, what else did you do after the body was taken off the wrecked boat?"

"As two of my men were taking the stretcher and body up the steep incline, I walked around the boat looking for any identifying markings. It was then that I discovered the all-important HIN #879 47654 0449, which was barely legible as was the boat's name *Arabella,* which would ultimately lead us to the craft's rightful owner."

"Bastard!" yelled Veronica, stunning the entire courtroom. Judge Horowitz, with apoplectic annoyance, grabbed his gavel, pounding the bench repeatedly. "Order, order! Lady, if you do anything like this again, I will have you taken outside the courtroom by the sergeant at arms. A repeat performance like this will get you barred from these proceedings permanently. Do you understand me?"

Veronica knew she was in trouble. After responding to the judge, she excused herself and walked out of the courtroom seeking to find a ladies' room.

Judge Horowitz rose from the bench. "Five-minute recess." Everyone was asked to rise as the judge headed for his chambers.

As soon as Veronica sat down on the stool, she retrieved a silver flask from the gigantic purse she always carried, taking a healthy portion of its alcoholic content. Next she resorted to a strong mouthwash on hand. She checked her makeup, touched up the rouge, and refreshed her lipstick before heading back to the courtroom. She made a final check on the seams of her hose before she walked down the deserted hallway.

Just then Judge Horowitz emerged back on the scene, and all were asked by Bailiff Butler to rise. Veronica couldn't help seeing Judge Horowitz looking her up and down. It didn't really intimidate her. She held her head up high and proudly, conveying a certain arrogance for which she was well known in her circles. *He is a bastard, and I don't give a hoot how you feel about it, Mr. Judge. You might do me a big favor by barring me from having to listen to what's to come.*

Hermione Grand didn't miss a beat. "Please, carry on, Commander."

"We transported the body of the young woman to the mortuary at the police station, Precinct #18, and turned it over to Coroner Fortran on duty on September 24, 1968—just to be precise. I believe it more appropriate for Dr. Fortran to testify as to his findings postmortem."

"You are correct in that assumption. I reserve the right to recall this witness later."

Judge Horowitz sat up straight. "The defense may cross-examine the witness."

"Defense has no questions for the witness at this time. Thank you, your Honor," said Max Weinstein.

"You may step down," said Judge Horowitz to the witness.

"Prosecution, you may call your next witness."

"Thank you, your Honor. I call to the stand Sergeant Beard-sley."

Tony Beardsley made his way to the front of the room,

wondering what he could add to the testimony already spelled out so thoroughly by Commander Shepherd.

"Will the witness please remain standing to be sworn in by the bailiff?"

Bailiff Butler addressed Sergeant Tony Beardsley. "Please raise your right hand. Do you swear to tell the truth, the whole truth, and nothing but the truth?" Beardsley hesitatingly placed his right hand on the Bible held in front of him; everyone on the force was aware that Tony was an avowed atheist.

"I do," said Sergeant Beardsley, who then walked very deliberately to the witness stand and sat down.

"Please state your full name."

"My name is Tony Arthur Beardsley. I'm a Sergeant with the San Diego PD, Precinct #18."

Prosecutor Hermione Grand could sense the hesitation evident in the demeanor of the next witness sitting in front of her. She decided to make it easy on him.

"You probably wonder why I called you to the stand. I just would like to know if you have anything to add to what Commander Shepherd told us."

"First, I concur with Chief Shepherd; it was a miracle that the craft survived the storm and succeeded in being washed ashore as totally demolished as she was; that is, both masts were razed and all rigging was ripped off the deck. The broken glass and pottery in the front of the inner chamber were to be expected. My thorough inspection of the portion of the hull past the bulkhead, where we located the body of the woman, indicated to me that no confrontations, attacks, sexual involvements, or any form of assault had taken place. The aura was one of total tranquility. It was almost eerie. Returning to the boat for our second search, we found some hair on a man's ball cap and a small, flat box, crumpled gift wrap, and a ribbon that had been tossed on the floor. The box could have held a necklace or similar piece of jewelry at one time. Nothing else of significance." Sergeant Beardsley took a deep breath. "That's all I have to add."

"Thank you, Sergeant, for your added testimony." Prosecutor Grand looked at Judge Horowitz and then at Max Weinstein: "I reserve the right to recall this witness later."

Judge Horowitz was totally involved. "The defense may cross-examine the witness."

"Defense has no questions for the witness at this time. Thank you, your Honor," said Max Weinstein.

"You may step down," said Judge Horowitz to the witness.

"Prosecution, you may call your next witness."

"Thank you, your Honor. I call to the stand Coroner Fortran."

Coroner Fortran walked to the front of the courtroom. In passing, he noted the dark figure seated in the very back, to the left of where he had been seated.

"Will the witness please remain standing to be sworn in by the bailiff?" said Judge Horowitz.

Bailiff Butler addressed Coroner Fortran. "Please raise your right hand. Do you swear to tell the truth, the whole truth, and nothing but the truth?" Fortran placed his right hand on the Bible held in front of him without any hesitation.

"I do," said Coroner Fortran, who then entered the witness stand and sat down.

"Please state your full name."

"My name is Archibald Andrew Fortran. I'm the coroner with the San Diego PD, Precinct #18."

Anyone present on this morning viewed this witness with particular interest. The courtroom artist had changed position, allowing her to sketch the man under most favorable lighting conditions on his face. Hermione Grand stood close to Dr. Fortran and addressed the witness.

"Dr. Fortran, please tell this Court in as great detail as possible what you found when you performed the autopsy on the alleged victim."

"The alleged victim was brought to the mortuary by Sergeants Beardsley and Townsend at 10:43 a.m. on the morning of September 24, 1968. The corpse had been placed on the stretcher, maintaining the position as closely as humanly possible in which she was discovered in the hull of the boat. The body was carefully shrouded, preventing contact by any flying insects. The body of the woman was fully clothed including underwear, stockings and shoes, and a rather fashionable, loosely fitting two-piece sports ensemble over an elegant white blouse. Before I proceeded with preparing the corpse for autopsy, I inspected the small pouch Sergeant Beardsley and Commander Shepherd discovered when they lifted the alleged victim off the floor of the boat's hull.

"Excuse me Ma'am, I need to take a drink of water." Fortran picked up the bottle of water he always carried with him and took a healthy slug.

"Please continue with your testimony," said Hermione Grand.

"Needless to say, I was wearing and changing gloves throughout the entire process. The pouch contained the woman's driver's license, a hundred dollars in various bills and some change, a couple of keys, a lipstick, and a typed note. The note read: 'The enclosed should take care of our little problem.'

It was unsigned. On the back of the note was the typed address of a doctor, George H. Harm, MD. Fertility Consultant (818) 747-4900. Commander Shepherd's secretary, Alice Walker, did some research on this person, and it is believed that the gentleman in question operates an abortion clinic in South Central Los Angeles. In view of my findings of the condition of the young woman, I can state with complete confidence that she never availed herself of the services of Dr. Harm. I believe pursuing this avenue of investigation would be fruitless."

Fortran stopped speaking. He was fully aware of the gasps detected by those in the courtroom. Even cool prosecutor Hermione Grand was momentarily taken aback. The dark figure in the back of the room was audibly sobbing.

Judge Horowitz rose from his chair. "I'm calling for a five-minute recess," and he walked slightly slouched toward his chambers.

Bailiff Butler called for all to rise as the judge vacated the bench. Most spectators and those directly involved in the proceedings elected to stand as if it were a seventh-inning stretch. Punctually as always, Judge Horowitz emerged from chambers and Bailiff Butler called for all to rise who were not standing. Peace and quiet at last returned to the courtroom.

"Please continue with your testimony," were the first words spoken by the prosecutor.

"She wasn't wearing any rings, but a stunning eighteen-karat gold charm bracelet was on her left wrist. One of the charms, a heart shape, bore the inscription 'With Love – HA III.'"

Veronica tapped Horatio on his right shoulder and pulled him slightly closer to her. She leaned into him and whispered: "You miserable prick stole that from me and gave it to that wench? It was a gift to me from you for my fiftieth birthday, a gift I paid for with my money. I accused Ping of having taken it. He vehemently denied having done so. I'm glad I didn't fire him. You are unbelievable!" Horatio sat up straight, totally ignoring Veronica.

Fortran continued. "Once fully stripped of her clothing, stockings, and shoes, I proceeded with the postmortem. I was particularly interested in discovering if the right hand of the woman so firmly fisted held anything within. I softened the tissue and discovered that the fist indeed contained a small object.

"What she clasped in her right hand was an empty vial. Upon testing it for residue, we discovered that it must have contained a dose of cyanide at one time. The use of cyanide by the person in question was confirmed by the presence of the poison on her lips and nostrils. Toxicological testing of her liver provided further evidence that the victim ingested cyanide. Based on our examinations of body temperature, rigor mortis, livor mortis (lividity), degree of putrefaction, stomach contents, and corneal cloudiness, we estimated that death occurred between twenty-four and thirty-six hours before our examination."

There was total silence in the courtroom, except for the soft sniffling taking place in the back. Judge Horowitz refrained from admonishing the darkly clad and veiled person. Fortran took another slug of water.

"According to the driver's license the young woman carried, she was born on October 23, 1934, meaning, she was about to celebrate her thirty-fourth birthday. She was not quite five months' pregnant. Her name was Juliana A. D. Knecht."

All present in the room had the same thoughts that had

crossed Commander Shepherd's mind when first learning of Coroner Fortran's discoveries on September 24. *Cyanide, keys, pregnant, a note! Who knows, someone may have forced her hand in taking the poison.*

At that moment, photographs taken of Juliana's face were projected on the large screen. Fortran proceeded: "We examined her body with extreme care. There was absolutely no evidence that Juliana was physically harmed or had defended herself against any kind of attacker. We paid particular attention to her fingernails, her torso, her breasts, and there were no signs she had been sexually assaulted. None whatsoever! Examining the fetus, it would have been a male.

"Nevertheless, a close search for other supporting evidence possibly present on the boat itself where she apparently died appeared to be advisable. Commander Shepherd heeded my advice and returned to the cutter for further investigation, which did not yield any significant evidence except a few hairs retrieved from a man's ball cap hanging from a nail in the hull of the boat. He also mentioned that they had overlooked a small, flat box, crumpled gift wrap, and a ribbon tossed onto the floor of the inner space. The box might have held a necklace or similar piece of jewelry at one time." Fortran's body language conveyed to the court that he viewed his testimony concluded.

Hermione Grand spoke: "Does that conclude your testimony, Sir?"

"Yes, Ma'am."

"I have a follow-up question. Did your forensic evaluations allow the assumption that the alleged victim could have died after the boat was stranded or possibly just prior to being washed ashore at Cabrillo National Monument?"

"The tests we conducted permit us to make the inference

that death indeed occurred after the boat was stranded at our shores or only within hours prior to that occurrence, the implication being that the alleged victim attempted to sail her heavily damaged vessel to safety; the latter being clearly subject to speculation."

"I have no more questions. Thank you, Coroner, for your testimony." Prosecutor Grand looked at Judge Horowitz and then at Max Weinstein: "I reserve the right to recall this witness later."

Judge Horowitz was evidencing a degree of tiredness. "The defense may cross-examine the witness."

"Thank you, your Honor," said Max Weinstein.

"Defense has only a few questions for the witness at this time. My questions pertain to the note to which you made reference, Dr. Fortran. Was the note typed on a particular kind of paper and was the note examined for the presence of any fingerprints?"

"The note was carefully examined. We detected a small area showing a particular watermark, which was photographed and enlarged. Our fingerprint specialist, Dr. Morris Finkelstein, reported the presence of two sets of fingerprints. One belonging to Ms. Knecht, the others, more pronounced, belonging to another person, unknown at this point in time."

"Thank you, Dr. Fortran. I have no further questions for the witness at this time but reserve the right for additional questioning at a later point. Thank you, your Honor," said Max Weinstein.

"You may step down," said Judge Horowitz to the witness.

Judge Horowitz resorted to the use of his gavel. "This court is now adjourned. We proceed with further testimony at nine o'clock tomorrow morning." He rose from his chair.

Bailiff Butler spoke: "All rise. Court is adjourned." Those who were watching the judges' exit with interest noticed that he was reaching to unbutton his judicial robing as he headed for his private chambers.

The darkly cloaked figure in the back of the courtroom was among the first to exit after adjournment had been announced. She was cause for speculation for most spectators as well as for those directly linked to the trial. Veronica looked at Horatio and then at Max Weinstein. "Were either of you aware of the lady in black with the severe veil? I noticed her after my interlude with Judge Horowitz and my quick getaway to the ladies' room. Talk about disguise. Makes me wonder who she is and why she is in attendance."

"I never saw her," said Max. "Neither did I," added Horatio. "Where was she sitting?"

"She sat in the last row of seats directly behind us. I couldn't help seeing her; the severity of her getup was such that I couldn't miss her. It will be interesting to see if she will be in attendance for the remainder of the trial. For now, let's get out of here as quickly as possible. I'm famished."

Max spoke up. "As we leave the courthouse, members of the media and the press may approach us. Do not make any statements. Keep them away from you and when asked to comment, simply state: "No comment!" and keep on walking toward our hotel. I'm beginning to think we would have been better off at a more distant location. Then we could just jump into our car or a cab and get away from these vultures. There are days when I absolutely hate the media."

"Yuck," said Horatio. "Just the thought of facing reporters makes me ill to my stomach. When I think what they did to me during my run for the Senate in '64, I don't even want to think about it."

"Oh, poor dear. If you hadn't always been such a schlemiel and constant cheat in our marriage, chasing every possible skirt all over the state, you would have nothing to hide and worry about. But you couldn't even keep your fly zipped and your filthy mouth shut when you were caught red-handed during the election. It was bad enough with all the stuff the media had on you from years past." Veronica kept pulling on her skirt, trying to flatten some of the wrinkles as she kept talking and walking.

Chapter 22

ARABELLA Davos Knecht was approached by one of the many reporters flooding the hallways of the courthouse and kept right on walking. She had purposely chosen not to wear heels, making sure she had good footing, allowing her to walk quickly. It helped that she regularly walked everyday of the week with the intent of staying in good physical shape. She had recently celebrated her fifty-eighth birthday and considered herself an attractive woman, but certainly not one who was looking to attract another man. She was never concerned about retaining a svelte figure but believed it to be important to keep moving and to stay healthy.

"What's your interest in the trial? What's your connection? Why the severe disguise?" Arabella ignored the woman reporter and raised her hand to hail a cab. She was fortunate that an alert cabbie spotted her and pulled up promptly at the curb. If the reporter could have seen Arabella's eyes, she would have been dead. There was murder in her eyes. She reached for the door handle, swiftly seated herself in the backseat of the cab, and pulled the door shut.

"Hilton, Southwest, please," was all she was capable of saying as she was catching her breath.

"Sorry, Ma'am. I feel for you. Some of these people are downright obnoxious. I see such scenes so often play out in front of the courthouse. All these reporters are interested in is to create headlines in their newspapers or get the attention of the public on the evening news on TV. They don't care about the person whose privacy they invaded.

"Here we are, Ma'am." He quickly glanced at his meter. "That will be one dollar fifty. Enjoy the rest of the day." Arabella handed him two bucks. He had stepped out of the cab and was holding the rear door open for his passenger. She was glad he was a simpatico sort. And then, she turned around. "What is your name? Do you have a business card? I may need your services at least twice a day for the next week or so."

"At your service; Julien Solomika. I'll be very pleased to chauffeur you whenever needed. Here is my business card. You can reach me at this number anytime. The dispatcher can get to me wherever I am."

"Please meet me at this entrance to the hotel tomorrow morning at eight-thirty and be at the courthouse by noon. I have no intention of staying any longer. Don't worry about having to wait for me; I will be delighted to pay you whatever it takes as long as I don't have to suffer being barraged by media people."

"Certainly, Ma'am. At your service." He bowed slightly at the waist. Arabella Davos Knecht, the epitome of grace and elegance, walked into the San Diego Hilton. *Quite the lady,* he thought, as his gaze followed her until she disappeared behind the darkened glass doors.

She had entered the hotel swiftly, briefly nodding a

greeting toward the porter who had held the door for her. Arabella headed straight for the bank of elevators, not making eye contact with anyone. She was not in the mood for idle chitchat. She retrieved her room key from her purse, entering her sizable and elegantly appointed room on the fifth floor of the hotel. She had a beautiful view of the harbor, noticing del Coronado in the faint distance.

"Phew!" she pulled off the cloche and veil. Next she shed her shoes and the three-quarter length black coat she wore over the stylish black silk dress. What she had worn she had chosen to disguise herself, as well as to show to the world that she was still in mourning for her one and only child, Juliana Arabella. She was thankful for the fresh air outside and opened a window. There was nothing to fear at this hotel and certainly not on the fifth floor.

"Oh, this feels so much better," she said out loud. Arabella sat down in a comfortable chair and put up her feet on the ottoman. *Thata girl. Relax. You may even order a cocktail from the bar. You deserve it after the events of this morning,* her brain was racing. The testimony by the last three witnesses had really gotten to her, especially the pronouncements by Coroner Fortran. *Whoever wrote that note?*

She remembered Commander Shepherd talking about it the night she learned from his lips of Juliana's death. She wished she had questioned Juliana on that fateful evening when she saw her last. She was aware that Juliana had recognized a certain person when leafing through those old photographs. But she didn't dare pose any questions; Juliana was always a very private individual. And now—it was too late. Juliana had been laid to rest at Forest Lawn weeks ago and could no longer speak for herself.

The gravesite had been beautifully laid out after the soil settled, and Juliana's full name had been added to the marker by Stonemason Herbert. He had charged her a pittance for what he did. The cemetery nursery had done a splendid job of reworking the gravesite, and she found all to her liking and satisfaction when she made a trip to Forest Lawn during Advent. She saw the promise of springtime, but wanted to be sure a colorful wreath would appear on Anton and Juliana's grave for the holidays.

She saw the grave in front of her mental eye and began to cry softly. All she could mumble was "My poor child, my poor child." She walked over to the side of her bed and picked up the phone.

"Please connect me to the hotel bar."

"Hilton, the Oroviso Bar. Jesus Antonero speaking. How may I help you?"

"This is Arabella Davos Knecht. I'm in room #508. Please make me a Rob Roy up—and have it brought to my room. Charge it to my bill, please. Thank you, Mr. Antonero."

"Coming up pronto, Ma'am!" She had hung up the phone.

She answered the door a few minutes later, tip in hand. A young, uniformed bellhop stood in front of her. "Here is your drink, Ma'am. I hope it is to your liking." He extended the silver tray holding the Rob Roy in a crystal snifter and a half dozen tastefully arranged petit fours. She was thankful to Jesus for his considerateness.

Arabella accepted the tray and handed the bellhop his well-deserved tip and smiled. "Thank you, young man, I'm sure I will enjoy this. Thank Jesus for me," she added, as she gently closed the door to her room. She retreated to her comfortable chair and ottoman and took her first sip. *Perfect! Just the way Anton used to make it for me.* She lifted her glass toward the large picture window: "Here's to both of you, my loves." She decided not to cry anymore, at least not for the remains of the evening. Of course, tomorrow was another day.

At the Wheatmark Hotel it was a different story. Max Weinstein had retreated to his room, seeking peace and quiet, wanting to go over the notes he made in preparation for the trial. He had looked over the list of prospective witnesses for the prosecution and knew that some of them would be more difficult to take than others. His biggest concerns were not with the witnesses lined up by Hermione Grand but the defendant whom he represented and his spouse.

After the brief confrontation between Veronica and Judge Horowitz, Max had warned her to be on guard. As soon as they had grabbed a quick bite to eat at the hotel café, he found a secluded corner, wanting to discuss courtroom etiquette with Veronica.

"No more outbursts in the courtroom. What you did this morning was totally out of line. It's not only offensive to our judge but may color the opinions of members of the jury. It's all a question of perception. I know Judge Horowitz very well and have seen him respond and react to this sort of undesirable behavior in his courtroom. If you want to remain seated in the courtroom during the trial, I urge you to control yourself. It doesn't help our cause."

"Tsk-tsk on me," as she was sipping her second sizable drink.

"Don't drink so much. We can't have another episode of you

being totally smashed. You need to be on your best behavior. You speak of Horatio's dark side and his peccadilloes. You've got your own shortcomings. Alcohol is no longer your friend; it makes you obnoxious, intolerant, and often not very pleasant to be with. Besides that, I can't have either of you sitting in the courtroom nodding off during court procedures. I saw that happening to you, Horatio, a few times this morning. While I've seen and heard Nathaniel Horowitz admonish jurors for nodding off—and rightfully so—he won't do that to you. But the image it conveys to the jurors is not one I want them to remember. I want both of you to watch how much you imbibe tonight and have a decent meal. I recommend that you refrain from going out and that you hit those pillows early and get a good night's sleep."

Horatio nodded. Veronica, of course, had to comment. "Yes, Papa Weinstein. Is that what a good Jewish wife would do?"

"Let's not even go there. And keep my good wife out of it. I'm not joking; I'm dead serious about what I just tried to get across to both of you. There's a lot at stake. I'm not a miracle worker. I would be a liar if I told you everything was just hunky-dory. They've got a lot of solid evidence against you, Horace. You are not off the hook yet. My reputation as an excellent criminal defense attorney precedes me, but as I said before, I don't walk on water."

Max Weinstein got up. "I'm off to my room. I'll take a quick power nap and then I want to work without being disturbed. I'll meet you in the hotel dining room at seven o'clock. Behave yourselves in the meantime." He walked toward the elevators. Mr. and Mrs. Alvis and he occupied two penthouse rooms on the 49th floor. *Classic Veronica; nothing but the best, he thought.*

As soon as Max had disappeared, Veronica confronted

Horatio. "He's right about not being a miracle worker and the prosecution having a pretty solid case against you. I'm curious to learn what kind of keys were in that pouch the woman carried with her. I hope to God they weren't keys to the *Horatio III* or some other place where you might have entertained your women. How stupid of you!" She swallowed the rest of her drink. "I won't have another one until we go out for dinner. I need to take a long nap.

"This morning was a very trying experience for me. First, that confrontation with Judge Horowitz, then seeing this dark figure sitting in the courtroom, and finally listening to that coroner. That really got to me. I hope to God they can't prove that you wrote that note and that you are the one who wound up killing that girl.

"I'm glad we have two queen beds in our room; I'm not sure I could sleep in the same bed with you any longer. I was almost tempted to get my own room. I only went for this arrangement at Max's recommendation. He thought if the press got wind of us having separate rooms, they'd have a field day with their innuendos and interpretations. Well, let's go. Get off your duff; I need that beauty nap—badly."

Chapter 23

ULRIKE Hammer drove home to her apartment in Glendale. It had been a full and trying day at her pharmacy. Some days she wished she didn't own her business. Having a nine-to-five job would have been easier. Standing on her legs for most of a given day was challenging. She was often subject to extreme pain in her upper right leg, still heavily scarred from the burns suffered in that tragic department store fire.

She had stopped for a few moments at Forest Lawn cemetery, having the need to commune with her dear deceased friend. The sun had just set and she knew she had to leave quickly before darkness set in. Looking around the site, faintly glowing in the dusk of the evening, she knew she was alone. Ulrike stepped to the right of the grave marker, having the need to touch it.

"I've honored your request and not opened the letter you entrusted to me. As you asked me in your cover note, I follow the evening news religiously. I read in the *LA Times* that the trial of a man by the name of Horatio Alvis III has begun. Due to a change of venue, the trial is held in San Diego. Honoring your request, I shall only open your letter if I'm inclined to believe the time has come to take certain actions." Ulrike began to sob as she walked away from Juliana's grave.

She drove away in a hurry, anxious to get to her home. Walking into the apartment, she made sure all three locks were secured and then tossed her keys on the kitchen counter. Her shoes kicked off and her warm jacket casually pitched on a nearby stool, she found rest in her Ekornes leather chair and ottoman. She looked down at herself. *Gosh, I must have been in a real hurry to get out of there. I even forgot to take off my lab coat,* she mused. She couldn't help seeing it. There it was, staring back at her, the envelope of the letter she had received in the mail on September 24, 1968. It was postmarked in Morro Bay and dated September 20, 1968. Ulrike opened the envelope, reading and rereading Juliana's cover note for the umpteenth time, never truly knowing what to make of it.

Dearest Ulrike,

I'm at the Morro Bay Yacht Club where I met my gentleman friend earlier. He left an envelope with me which I'm not supposed to open until I am alone. The seas are a bit choppy; nevertheless, I intend to go out for a boat ride. I've sailed that craft in all sorts of weather and am looking forward to the challenge. There are too many question marks in my life these days, and I believe you are the only one whom I can trust with my unusual request. There might come a time when the evening news will be of special interest to you. Read the enclosed letter _only_ under certain circumstances. You will know when to do so. Use this instrument wisely. Much love,

Your friend Juliana

Whenever she read that last phrase, it totally puzzled her. Ulrike picked up the enclosure and shook it. From the weight of it, it was either a lengthy note or was written on much heavier paper than the cover note. While she was desiring to open the letter as often as she held it in her hands during the last three months since Juliana's death, she had not succumbed to the temptation of reading its content and respected her friend's wishes, expressed perhaps just hours before she died.

At this moment, she decided to fix herself a drink and turned on the evening news.

Under the rubric of state news, the announcer spoke briefly of the Horatio Alvis III trial taking place in a San Diego courtroom. Testimony by early witnesses was inconclusive, with trial to continue Tuesday morning. She was hoping for better reportage in the next day's *LA Times*.

Chapter 24

THE air was crisp under a bright blue sky as Max Weinstein, his client Horatio Alvis, and his client's wife Veronica walked briskly toward the courthouse in San Diego. All prepared to be accosted by reporters, they were pleased to have reached the courthouse without confrontations with paparazzi.

Walking down the long corridors was another story. Veronica found it most annoying when some of the reporters actually touched her, trying to elicit any kind of response. She had paid attention to Max. Hiding her eyes behind most-fashionable and very dark glasses, she glared at her nemeses: "No comment! Beat it!" She would keep right on walking, her high heels clicking loudly across the highly polished marble floors.

Veronica turned to Max and Horatio; "I don't know how many days I can go through this, and it will only get worse. These people are insatiable. I can't wait for the whole thing to be over."

"You don't have to be on-site. Neither Max nor the prosecutor have indicated they want you on the witness stand.

And even if they did, you have the right to refuse. So, suit yourself," said Horatio.

"That would be the easy way out. I would rather hear some of this stuff firsthand than regurgitated by the media. I guess I'll just have to learn to live with this whole media circus."

All were relieved when they entered the hallowed quiet of the courtroom. Veronica quickly glanced over her left shoulder, noticing again the dark figure seated in the back row of the chamber. *Who is she?* She didn't voice. The mystery of this person's appearance bothered her immensely. *Was she just a spectator, or a prospective witness?*

Punctually at nine o'clock, Judge Horowitz emerged from his chambers. Bailiff Butler did his routine.

"Please rise. The Court of the Ninth Judicial Circuit, Criminal Division, is now in session, the Honorable Judge Nathaniel Horowitz presiding. Judge Horowitz addressed the Court:

"Ladies and gentlemen of the Jury, you are still under oath. Please conduct yourselves in accordance with the instructions given to you by me yesterday."

Judge Horowitz faced Hermione Grand: "Ms. Grand, please call your next witness."

"Thank you, your Honor. I call to the stand Dr. Horatio Alvis IV."

Horatio Alvis Jr. approached the front of the courtroom.

"Will the witness please remain standing to be sworn in by the bailiff?"

Bailiff Butler looked at Dr. Alvis. "Please raise your right hand. Do you swear to tell the truth, the whole truth, and nothing but the truth?" Horatio Alvis IV appeared to be totally relaxed and at ease, almost blasé, an astute participant might have observed. He placed his hand on the Bible without hesitation.

"I do," said Horatio IV, who then walked to the witness stand and sat down.

Hermione Grand approached this next witness with an élan for which she was well known in judicial circles.

"Please state your full name." Surprising herself, Hermione Grand was nearly into the man's face. Her eyes appeared to pierce through the young man. Horatio, ever so slightly, backed away from her.

"My name is Horatio Alvis IV, MD."

"I understand you are a doctor of internal medicine and presently practicing at Bayside Hospital in San Luis Obispo. Is this correct?"

"Yes, Madam Prosecutor."

"I believe you are the son of the defendant and were advised by counsel that you may elect not to testify for the prosecution. However, I do appreciate your willingness to do so in the name of justice. Please tell us about your relationship to Juliana A. D. Knecht. I'm particularly interested in how and where you met."

"I met Juliana during my third year in medical school. That would have been 1958 to 1959, somewhere in that vicinity. I had decided to pursue a non-glamorous career in internal medicine, and Juliana was seriously planning to get her degree in pharmacology. We were casual luncheon companions and now and then shared dinner at a nicer restaurant. Unlike many of our classmates, neither Juliana nor I were seriously in pursuit of sexual partners. We enjoyed our friendship, attended a few concerts and plays, and discovered in time a mutual interest in sailing. After I graduated from medical school, my father made me a present of the aging sailboat he replaced with a much larger and fancier yacht. Actually, my mother had bought the *Horatio III* for my father.

"Both vessels were kept at the Morro Bay Yacht Club. After both of us finished medical school, we continued seeing each other on occasion. Juliana liked sailing the old cutter, and I made sure she became confidant in handling the small vessel. Eventually, I gave Juliana free reign and access to the craft; she could come and go as she pleased. Myself, I became so immersed in my medical practice, leaving me little time to pursue outside interests. Juliana, on the other hand, fell in love with sailing the *Arabella* and took her out to sea frequently. Now and then she'd call and thank me for making the small sailboat so readily available to her. We rarely saw each other in the last few years. I was shocked to learn of Juliana's untimely death when I was interrogated by Commander Shepherd last September. I believe we spoke on September 26, a Thursday."

Hermione Grand looked at Dr. Alvis. "Do you by any chance recall when last you saw Juliana?"

"Actually, I do. I was leaving our church after Epiphany services. That would make it January sixth of last year. I wasn't even aware that she attended my church. We stopped at a Subway and grabbed a quick bite to eat. We talked perhaps for an hour. She told me she was seeing a mature man who was several years older than she. I wished her the best as we parted. That was the last time I saw Juliana A.D. Knecht."

"I won't ask you to describe your whereabouts on the night of Sunday, September 22, 1968. Having read the detailed responses you gave Commander Shepherd, and being able to account for the time you spend at the hospital and with your friend, I believe you have a sufficient alibi.

"Madam Prosecutor, I would like to hear where Dr. Alvis was on the night in question and what he did on that day," intervened Judge Horowitz.

"Dr. Alvis, please continue with your testimony," instructed Hermione Grand, Prosecutor.

"That Sunday, September 22, 1968, I slept in late, had breakfast in my apartment, went for a run for a good hour, and then took a much-needed shower. I swung by the hospital to catch up on some paperwork. I was at the office from about one until five-ish. Staff on duty could clearly vouch for me, although many chose not to come in because of the increasing winds. Normally I grab a bite to eat for lunch at one of the little bistros near the hospital. However, on that Sunday, because of all the rain and hail, I stayed in and had some of the delectable hospital fare. People must have seen me in the cafeteria.

"When one of the nurses on duty called it a day shortly after five, I contacted a buddy of mine and met him at the *Cat & Mouse* pub to shoot the breeze over a couple brews and a light supper. I hate eating alone. Matt Lawler, MD, has been a good friend since high school. We graduated from different medical schools but always remained in close touch. He dropped me off at my pad close to ten o'clock. I set my alarm after I entered my apartment, took another shower, and went straight to bed. I left for my office at seven-thirty the next morning. All cars entering and leaving our underground garage are monitored by a gatekeeper. I received the call from the Morro Bay Yacht Club just before noon on Monday morning. Whoever I spoke to was positive that the moorings were torn by the high winds that pounded the waters."

"Thank you, Dr. Alvis," spoke Judge Horowitz.

"You are welcome, your Honor."

Somewhat flummoxed by the judge's interjection, Hermione Grand stated:

"You have anything to add to your statements, Dr. Alvis?"

"No. I believe I have stated all that is pertinent to my recollections."

Judge Horowitz scratched his chin. "The defense may cross-examine the witness."

"Defense has no questions for the witness. Thank you, your Honor," said Max Weinstein.

"You may step down," said Judge Horowitz to the witness.

"Prosecution, you may call your next witness."

"Thank you, your Honor. I call to the stand Gerald Smothers, Morro Bay Harbormaster."

Gerald Smothers approached the front of the courtroom.

"Will the witness please remain standing to be sworn in by the bailiff?"

Bailiff Butler looked at Gerald Smothers. "Please raise your right hand. Do you swear to tell the truth, the whole truth, and nothing but the truth?" Smothers laid his fleshy right hand on top of the Bible presented to him by the bailiff.

"I do," said Gerald Smothers, who then walked to the witness stand and sat down.

Hermione Grand approached this next witness.

"Please state your full name."

"My name is Gerald Jerome Smothers."

"My records indicate that you are the harbormaster for Morro Bay. How long have you been in this position? What exactly is the function of a harbormaster?

"I have been harbormaster in Morro Bay since May 1st of

1927. At the time, the community was flush with money and built a beautiful facility to accommodate my offices and offices for my staff relatively close to the Morro Bay Yacht Club. I was a commissioned officer in the Navy during WWI and subsequently spent a few years at sea in the Merchant Marines. The job of harbormaster was a natural for me. I have never loved any job any better. I must have loved it, doing the same job for forty years."

Hermione Grand smiled approvingly. "What all does the position of harbormaster entail?"

"As harbormaster, I provide information re local safety issues; oversee navigational aids within my jurisdiction—i.e., our particular port; coordinate actions dictated by emergencies; oversee pilot services; and sometimes inspect vessels as to their cargo and/or soundness of the vessels themselves. I'm in constant touch with weather services and am responsible for disseminating critical alerts assuring safety in harbor territory. In conjunction with local law enforcement, my duties may cover the investigations of criminal acts, immigration, as well as environmental and pollution issues."

"It was then in the investigation of an alleged crime that Commander Shepherd interrogated you on September 27 of last year. Is this correct? Do you recall the information you provided to the Commander?"

"Yes, I do. Commander Shepherd and Sergeant Beardsley were particularly interested in my assessment and recall of the weather conditions on Sunday, September 22. It was a nasty Pacific storm; we had twenty- to thirty-foot waves, pouring rain, and damaging hail. The harbor was a disaster. Many small vessels were thrown ashore. Boat owners residing in distant places were not aware of the damage that was done to their properties. The following day, the place was teeming with insurance agents scrambling to settle with their respective clients. Those were some of the worst days and nights I recall since becoming harbormaster forty years ago."

"You have anything to add to your statements?" asked the prosecutor.

"No. I believe I have stated all that is pertinent to your questions."

Judge Horowitz looked at the harbormaster: "The defense may cross-examine the witness."

"Defense has no questions for this witness. Thank you, your Honor," said Max Weinstein.

"You may step down," said Judge Horowitz to the witness.

"Prosecution, you may call your next witness."

"Thank you, your Honor. I call to the stand Commodore Ari Konstantinopolis."

Commodore Konstantinopolis approached the front of the courtroom.

"Will the witness please remain standing to be sworn in by the bailiff?"

Bailiff Butler glanced at the decorated uniform of Commodore Ari Konstantinopolis. "Please raise your right hand. Do you swear to tell the truth, the whole truth, and nothing but the truth?" Commodore Konstantinopolis for a moment hesitated to place his hand on the Bible presented to him by the bailiff.

"I do," said Ari Konstantinopolis, who then walked to the witness stand and sat down.

Hermione Grand approached this next witness. So far, he

was the most handsome man she had beheld on a witness stand in a long time. But, no matter how handsome, he was still just a witness needing to do his job for her.

"Please state your full name."

"My name is Adonis Ari Konstantinopolis." Hermione winced at the mention of the name "Adonis."

"My records indicate that you are currently CEO of the Morro Bay Yacht Club. How long have you held this position? What exactly are your functions as CEO for the yacht club?

"I served in the US Navy during WWI. I graduated from the Naval Academy in Annapolis in 1926 and took a position with the yacht club early in 1927. I held various positions within the organization until the bombing of Pearl Harbor in December 1941. I volunteered to rejoin the Navy and did a relatively short stint mostly shuffling papers in DC. I was honorably discharged for a second time in 1944. At forty-five, I would not be considered for active duty. Having fallen in love with the California climate, I returned to Morro Bay. I've held the position of Commodore since 1954.

"As Commodore, I'm the principal officer of the club. My duties are to set the direction for the club, and I'm responsible for its organization and management; that means, subordinates in charge of boating facilities, dining and social facilities, maintenance, and so forth report directly to me. I pride myself on knowing most members of the club, their respective vessels, and being out and about most days; I know what's going on out there."

Hermione Grand signaled her aide to activate the projector. A retouched and enlarged photograph taken from Juliana's driver's license was projected onto the courtroom screen. "Have you ever seen or known this woman?"

"Yes! As I told Commander Shepherd during his interrogation, I've seen the young woman on several occasions. Quite a number of years ago—don't ask me exactly what year—I saw this woman palling around with young Horatio Alvis. I saw them together in our dining room, and on other occasions he was showing her how to sail the craft that is now in question. Young Alvis received the small boat as a present from his father upon graduating from medical school. Mrs. Alvis acquired the *Horatio III*, a much larger vessel, which is also moored at our yacht club. The boat was moored close to the entrance to the harbor and not seen by too many regular visitors.

"More recently, I saw the young woman on a few occasions earlier this year in the company of Horatio Alvis III. Apparently, he entertained her for dinner on his yacht, the *Horatio III*."

"What can you tell us about the events of September 22, 1968? Did you see the woman in question and/or Alvis III or Alvis IV on that specific day?"

"I'm sorry to say I did not lay eyes on any of the three on that day. It was utter pandemonium in this place trying so save as many vessels as possible from the storm. Most people who were present that day were hiding behind face protectors, scarves, and bulky jackets and wraps. All of us were glad we survived the storm in as good a shape as we did. Only the next day did we become aware how many smaller vessels had been impacted by the storm."

"Was it on Monday, September 23, that you became aware that the sailboat *Arabella* was missing?"

"Yes, and I called Dr. Horatio Alvis IV later that morning advising him of the missing boat."

"In your professional opinion, is it possible that the

mooring cables were torn and the craft was forced out of the harbor by the storm?"

"Yes, it is a good possibility that the moorings were torn by the storm. It probably would not have happened had the boat been located closer to the inner harbor. Where it was, there was full impact from wind and the high seas. I'm amazed that she made it all the way to San Diego and didn't sink."

"You have anything to add to your statements?" asked the prosecutor.

"No. I believe I have answered your questions to the best of my recollection."

Judge Horowitz focused on the heavily decorated uniform of the last witness: "The defense may cross-examine the witness."

"Defense has no questions for this witness. Thank you, your Honor," said Max Weinstein.

"You may step down," said Judge Horowitz to the witness.

"Prosecution and defense, please approach the bench."

Judge Horowitz bent down and spoke quietly to Hermione Grand and Max Weinstein: "I'm not certain what's wrong with me, but I am experiencing some severe chest pains. I need to adjourn court for today and subject myself to an emergency examination."

As Grand and Weinstein returned to their tables, Judge Horowitz lifted the gavel. "Court is adjourned. We'll reconvene tomorrow at nine o'clock."

Bailiff Butler asked all to rise. Everyone in the courtroom was watching Judge Horowitz clutching his chest as he turned toward his chamber. Within seconds of adjournment, those who were leaving the confines of the courtroom became aware of sirens blaring outside the building.

✕

Arabella was the first to step out of the courthouse. She was pleased to see Julien Solomika and his splendid cab waiting for her by the curb. A reporter approached her from the right. She waved her gloved hand furiously in the man's direction. "Just leave me be; you are a pestilence on mankind!" She was thankful to Julien for having watched the whole scene. He was standing by the rear right door holding it open for her. Once she was safely seated in the car she smiled at Julien. "Thank you; you are a godsend. You are worth every cent in gold."

"Wouldn't that be nice. I'm afraid they have robbed Fort Knox blind. Entirely my pleasure to serve you, Ma'am. Whereto this afternoon?"

"Right now, please take me back to the hotel. I may have a bite of lunch in my room. I will call you this evening and have you drive me to a small but nice restaurant not too far away. If you are free this afternoon, I'm planning a little excursion. I need to see something with my own eyes. Would you mind driving me to Point Loma at the Cabrillo National Monument?"

"Not at all, Ma'am. Are you interested in seeing the old lighthouse? It is quite the tourist attraction."

"Oh, no! I've seen my share of lighthouses. I wish to see the shoreline in that vicinity. Is this a problem for you?"

"I will be delighted to drive you to the park. I know a pretty direct route; visitors to the city often wish to be taken to the Cabrillo statue and the old lighthouse. What time would you like me to call for you?"

"I don't want to make it too late since the sun sets shortly after five this time of year. How long does it take to drive to the lighthouse?"

"The way I know, about forty-five minutes, the most. Toward evening it may take an extra fifteen minutes. You pick the time since you know what you want to see."

"Make it two-thirty sharp, Mr. Solomika."

"Oh, Ma'am, please make it Julien. No one calls me by my Greek handle. I'll be waiting for you. Is there anything we need to take along on this outing?"

"Nothing that I know of today. We shall see. I'll be waiting for you by the front door."

Julien helped her out of the car, waving at her as she walked toward the hotel. He couldn't believe his good fortune. Arabella decided to stop and speak with the concierge. "May I see your menu for room service, please? I'm pressed for time and would like just something little for my noon repast."

"Certainly, Mrs. Knecht. I'll have the menu sent up to your room. Have a delightful afternoon."

The friendly bellhop delivered the menu within minutes of Arabella's arrival at room #508. She quickly glanced at the choices. "Why don't you make it half a Reuben on rye and a small cup of clam chowder. I prefer the Manhattan style. Thank you, young man."

"I'll be back shortly with your order."

"Thank you, that will be lovely."

Seeing herself in the mirror, she opted to change her clothes from the funerary look to something more cheerful and practical for what she had planned for the afternoon. She wasn't quite sure what to expect, but an inner voice had been urging her to view the place where Juliana Arabella had been found.

Her lunch arrived promptly. She rewarded the bellhop with

a deserving tip and then proceeded to enjoy the light meal she had ordered. She looked at her watch. *No need to wolf this down; it's not healthy for you. What would you do if you choked? So, enjoy this meal in peace and quiet. Lord knows what the afternoon and the next few days shall bring.* Now and then she had to have these little talks with herself.

Yes, she was casually dressed for the afternoon outing but certainly did not look sloppy. Sloppy, slovenly, and sleazy were not descriptors that would ever be associated with Arabella Davos Knecht. She was always a classy lady.

She was ready to walk out of the Hilton at the agreed time. Arabella was punctual, as was Julien. He helped her into the cab, and she nodded her appreciation for his courtesies. As soon as he had slipped behind the wheel, he turned back to her. "Make yourself comfortable and enjoy the ride. You'll get to see some pretty sites as soon as we are out of the downtown area. You mind sharing with me what interests you at Cabrillo National Monument? Is it the statuary at Point Loma?"

"No! It isn't any statuary. There's a scuttled sailboat on the beach way below the lighthouse. I don't even know if there is a way for you to drive within relative close proximity to the strand. I've never been anywhere near this place. You have to be patient with this old woman, but it is very important to me to face this reality."

"Not to worry. There is a manageable service road that goes down to the shore. We certainly can make it within fifty or seventy-five feet to the beach. It's a different approach than coming down from the lighthouse. Some visitors like to use the beach and get there using the service road rather than the paved road that takes you to the old lighthouse."

"I trust you completely."

Forty-five minutes later, Julien pulled over to the side of the road. "That is the beach that lies directly at the foot of the lighthouse. If you look up over your right shoulder, you should be able to see it. It's quite an incline to go up there."

And then she looked to her left with the beach clearly in front of her. High tide was coming in, but the object of her interest was securely lying on the sand, not to be disturbed by the tide. It must have been the stormy sea that had pushed the boat so much farther ashore on that fateful day last September. She finally found her voice and spoke. "Julien, would you indulge this foolish old woman and walk with me to that stranded boat you see lying on the beach."

"No, not at all. A little bit of exercise will be good for me."

He helped her out of the car. Arabella retrieved a collapsible cane from her purse and was not ashamed to use it. "Smart lady! I should have thought of that. Those things are darn handy. Nevertheless, hold on to my right arm. That way you'll be perfectly safe. Would you like to share with me what this is all about?"

"Of course not. You are my accomplice. That sailboat, lying on its side, is the boat that brought my dead daughter Juliana A. D. Knecht to these shores. The boat survived the ride in stormy seas from Morro Bay sometime between September 20 and September 24 of last year; my daughter did not. Her body was found in the hull of the ship. Apparently, she was murdered by someone giving her cyanide. I'm convinced the man whose trial I've been attending is the guilty party."

"Wow! I had no idea. Be careful where you are walking. Hold on tight. Wow! I can't really blame you for wanting to view this scene. Looks like the wind has torn away at the yellow tape delineating it as a crime scene."

"I have no need to climb aboard but want to walk around it. It holds good and mostly bad memories for me."

"How's that possible? Good memories?"

"Time has a way of changing our perceptions," said Arabella and continued talking.

"Thanks for bringing me here to see this." Slowly she walked on the soft sand, taking care not to touch the torn yellow tape. When she reached the stern, tears came into her eyes.

"Can you make out the name of the boat?"

Julien moved closer and played with his eyeglasses; perhaps they were not properly seated. "I believe it reads *Arabella*; is that correct?"

"Yes, that is the name of this boat. Not quite forty years ago, I was in love with a man and I was in love with sailing. My parents couldn't afford to have or keep a boat. My lover could. He bought this boat and named it for me. Not long after he acquired the vessel, he met another woman, a woman of elegance and substance. Our relationship ended. I was young and eventually got over the hurt. I discovered that other mothers had nice sons too. So, you see—this sailing craft carried some good and some bad memories with it. There's a lot more but it will have to wait until this trial is over."

At that very moment, Arabella knew exactly what needed to be done, and she was determined to carry out her plan no matter what might happen during the trial. In the end, she would triumph.

"Let's head back, Julien. The sun is about to set. I'm glad you knew of this access road. I would hate having to climb that steep hill up to the lighthouse. When we get back to the Hilton, I would like you to wait. I need to slip into something a bit more dressy. It won't take me long. I hate to be nosy? You are not wearing a wedding band. I know lots of men don't. By any chance, are you unattached?"

"As a matter of fact, I am. I was married, but my wife died of cancer ten years ago. I've never met another woman I wanted to be with. Perhaps I didn't look hard enough."

"That's just like me; my dear Anton has been gone for almost twenty-three years. I've never wanted to be with another man; he spoiled me too greatly." She took a deep breath.

"How would you like to join me and have dinner with me tonight. I suppose you are on duty with your cab and can't afford to lose all kinds of business while entertaining me over dinner?"

"Not at all. I'm not beholden to anyone. The car is mine, and I'm my own little company. I just work with a telephone service that functions as my dispatcher. If I sign off, that's it for the day. I'm delighted to accompany you to dinner. You have any particular preferences? There are lots of choices, Mrs. Knecht."

"Oh, please, Julien. Make it Arabella. I don't stand on such formality any longer. It's something my dear Juliana taught me."

"OK, Arabella, that works for me. I must tell you, I'm in love with your name; it lilts right off my tongue. Are you by any chance familiar with Richard Strauss's opera *Arabella*? It's one of my favorites."

"I've heard of it but have never seen it. Let's chat more about it over dinner. Obviously, I have access to good seafood and oriental cuisine where I live. I love Italian. What do you feel like having? You are the one who has been working. It's your choice."

"Great! Italian it is. Good choice. What time would you like me to fetch you?"

"How about seven? It will give me a chance to catch the evening news. Perhaps I'll learn what happened to the judge. When he adjourned court today, it looked like the dear man was having a heart attack. Wouldn't that be the pits? That would really be a monkey wrench."

"Let's hope not. I'll see you at seven o'clock. I know you'll love *Cucina Italiana.*"

⋈

Arabella quickly slipped into a colorful silk print, deciding to wear medium heels to give her just a tad more height. Julien was rather tall. She flipped on the TV not wanting to miss the local news. And there it was:

Judge Nathaniel Horowitz had to adjourn the Alvis III trial prematurely today because of experiencing an apparent heart attack. He was taken to the San Diego Medical Center for evaluation. It was determined that Judge Horowitz did not suffer a heart attack but was diagnosed with a severe case of food poisoning. He will be discharged from the facility on Thursday morning. The Alvis trial is to resume on Friday at nine o'clock.

Arabella was elated. She could use a couple of days of retreat from the Alvis affair. Having dinner with a handsome gentleman was the tonic she needed. She was looking forward to dining with Julien.

Julien's eyes popped. Arabella had casually thrown a dark ranch mink stole over her shoulders, showing much of the impressionistic silk print of her dress. As she walked briskly toward him, Julien didn't know at first what to say. He decided not to make it "wow," not wanting to appear like some horny teenager. As he seated her in the front passenger seat, he merely said: "Lovely, and no more talk of foolish old woman. You are neither."

Now it was Arabella's turn to blush. "Thank you, Julien. That was sweet of you to say. I really am looking forward to this dinner. And guess what? I'm free of the trial until Friday. Judge Horowitz didn't have a heart attack but suffered from food poisoning. He'll be back on the bench by Friday. I'm sure all who are involved are taking a breather. But, no more talk about the trial. I want to enjoy the evening."

They were seated at an elegant table at the *Cucina Italiana.* "Would you care for a drink, Arabella?" He still had to get used to calling her by that sensuous name.

"I would enjoy a Rob Roy—up. Anton was great at making those for me."

Julien turned to the waiter. "Please let us have two Rob Roys—*up!* We'll take a look at the menu. Thank you."

The drinks were presented promptly. "Give us a few minutes to order. Thank you."

Arabella studied the lined face of her handsome Greek who still had a full head of wavy gray hair. *What are you thinking, Arabella? Are you losing your mind? You've been a widow for twenty-three years. What's getting into you? My God, you are acting like a teenager in hormone warfare.*

"Where are you, Arabella? I know you are not with me?"

"As a matter of fact, I was too much with you. That's just it. I haven't felt this way since Anton died." She blushed. "Forgive me, I am a foolish old woman." Julien realized what was happening; even he had felt some stirrings he hadn't experienced in more than ten years. He lifted his glass toward Arabella.

"Let's drink to new beginnings." Arabella smiled.

"L'Chaim—to life! I love that expression," and she took a sip from her drink. When she set down her crystal glass, she reached across the table and gently touched his hands. She had forgotten how good it felt to touch another human being, how good it felt to reach out to a loving man.

Dinner was clearly a success. The ambiance of the restaurant and the food was perfect. As Julien held Arabella's hand walking out of *Cucina Italiana*, he recalled her toast. She was right, he needed to start thinking about being alive and to grasp at the opportunity for a new life, a new beginning.

He waved at the parking attendant. "Please bring my car around; it's that black Mercedes over there." Arabella didn't say a word and just smiled after Julien had made sure she was safely seated in his car. He pressed a five-dollar bill into the hand of the boy and thanked him for his service. *L'Chaim* kept ringing in his ears.

Pulling up in front of the Hilton, Arabella looked at him quizzically.

"Are you up to a nightcap? Jesus is a wonderful bartender. He'll be delighted to fix us another Rob Roy. I got the feeling you liked my poison."

"Are you certain? Aren't we rushing things?"

"How much time do we have at our ages? I didn't ask you to get into bed with me; I just asked you if you would care to have another drink. It would give us a chance to talk in private and perhaps get to know one another."

"I told you, you are not a foolish old woman—and indeed, you are not. You are neither foolish nor old as I said before. You are elegant, charming, and thankfully, full of life. I would love to have that Rob Roy with you."

He helped Arabella out of the car and turned the Mercedes over to the parking attendant. "Put it in long-term parking; I may stay the night." She hadn't heard what he said; the traffic noise was too overpowering. He took her left arm lightly and walked her by the concierge and toward the bank of elevators. "Which floor are we on?"

"I'm on floor five in room #508." I always have an "8" somewhere in my room numbers and would never stay on the 13th floor or in room 1313 because of my mother. She was terribly superstitious. It must have rubbed off."

"What's the bit with those numbers?"

"Eight stands for 'infinity,' as in 'forever,' and thirteen is generally known as an unlucky number, as in "Friday the 13th."

"Got it. Well, let's see if room #508 spells infinity for us." He pressed her hand lightly and called for the elevator.

Chapter 25

THE phone rang in Max Weinstein's penthouse suite at five-thirty in the afternoon. He had been deep in thought, seriously debating whether to put Horatio on the witness stand. He picked up the phone.

"Bailiff Butler speaking. I've been in touch with Judge Horowitz. Fortunately, he did not have a heart attack but suffered with an extreme case of food poisoning. He has requested to advise you, Ms. Hermione Grand, and all jurors of his disposition. He will be discharged from the hospital on Thursday, and trial proceedings in the Alvis III case shall resume Friday morning at nine. I would like to suggest that you and Ms. Grand advise your respective witnesses of the altered calendar. While these changes are subject to discussion in the media, a personal phone call to your witnesses is recommended. You have any questions, Sir?"

"Do I assume correctly that you have already contacted Ms. Grand and all jurors with this information?"

"Yes, Sir, I have, and Ms. Grand will phone all witnesses on her list. Anything else?"

"No! Thanks for getting in touch with me."

"You're welcome. See you in court Friday morning."

Max picked up some papers. *Guess we bit that bullet.* He dialed the number of Horatio and Veronica's room.

"Horatio Alvis speaking."

"Hi, it's Max. Hope I didn't awaken Veronica from her nap."

"No, we turned the phone off in the bedroom. I'm just reading the paper and got to the phone on the first ring. What's up, Max?"

"Just had a call from Bailiff Butler. The judge is OK; it was food poisoning rather than his heart. We'll have two days of a reprieve. The trial will resume on Friday at nine. This will give us a chance to discuss a few things. Are you still sure you want to be my one and only witness? As I told you before, I'm generally not in favor of putting a defendant on the stand. You'll be under oath and obliged to truthfully answer any questions fired at you by me, the prosecutor, and even the judge. Do you fully understand what I'm trying to tell you?"

"I do, Max. I'll slip out and come over to your pad rather than talking on the phone. I'm almost paranoid these days about telephone conversations, always wondering if I'm spied upon. Ever since that run for the Senate, I distrust everything. I'll be right over after scribbling a note for Veronica, letting her know where I am when she wakes up."

Horatio had put on comfortable jeans and a lightweight pullover. At sixty-two, he still cut a pretty good figure. Veronica had always insisted on his regularly working out in their gym, reminding him constantly: "Why waste all this fantastic exercise equipment we bought." As he was passing a full-length mirror in the hallway, he approved of his svelte bod.

He knocked on Max's door and was admitted immediately.

"Come in. Glad to see you made yourself a bit more comfortable. I got rid of my tie the minute I walked into my room. Of course, I wouldn't dream of appearing before Judge Horowitz in anything but appropriate attire. Grab a chair and let's talk. You've heard me say this before; I don't want any surprises. We want to be up-front with the fact that you knew Juliana in a casual way and that you met her through your son. You were aware of their friendship and her interests in sailing. You saw her occasionally at the Morro Bay Yacht Club because of both your boats being moored there. I'm sure you will be asked again if you saw her close to the time that she disappeared. You are absolutely positive you didn't run into her at the yacht club, let's say between Friday and Monday of that weekend?"

"I know I was in Morro Bay that Sunday because I took care of Ernest. To be honest with you, I'm all confused about that horrible Sunday. I may have run into her in that mad crowd. I'm no longer totally sure. It's a weekend I'd rather forget. There were so many things happening all around me; I cannot seem to separate fact from fiction."

"You better not make those kinds of statements on the witness stand. Grand and the judge will tear you to pieces. Like I told you yesterday, you need to watch what you are drinking and keep your head clear. You must be completely with it when I put you up on that stand. Any sort of dubious comments or statements you make open the door for questions by the prosecutor and judge. I won't press you any harder today, but you need to sit down quietly and think this through. Try to recall those days and perhaps even jot down some notes getting your facts in order. 'Maybes' and 'not sures' and those kinds of statements don't cut it with those people. They want 'yes' and 'no' answers and nothing in between. I'll let you go.

Order coffee and dessert for Veronica and yourself and relax. And make some notes. And whatever you do, don't get into arguments and fights with your wife. She'll really get you all confused."

"Good suggestions. I'll see what I can do." He walked away from Max, trying to get things straight in his head. He was fully aware of not having told Max the truth. Lying was tricky business; sooner or later he would pay the price for a life lived in deceit.

Chapter 26

ARABELLA awakened to bright sunshine. She had pleasant dreams, although she couldn't exactly recall any details. In a bit of a fog, she glanced at her alarm clock and realized it was past nine o'clock. *Oh, my God. I should be at the courthouse.* And then she remembered that it was only Wednesday, January 15. She didn't have to don her courtroom attire until Friday. She had two full days to enjoy herself in San Diego. She decided she would order an Espresso and a delectable croissant from Jesus; he was in charge of everything that had to do with food and drink. Reaching for the phone, she noticed the blinking red light. *I wonder who left me a message?* It was Prosecutor Hermione Grand confirming what she already knew. *Funny, I hadn't noticed that flashing light last night. I must have been too fascinated with Julien.*

Having taken the first sip of her regular morning stimulus, she picked up the phone. A smile crossed her face, recalling the enjoyable evening she had spent with a new man in her life.

"Hallo Julien, I hope I'm not waking you. I know it was

after midnight when I finally let you go. I had a perfectly wonderful evening."

"So did I, my dear. Great conversations and so much fun discovering things about each other. It took me back forty-some years when I met my first love. I can't even remember her name. But she was pretty, and she loved to talk. I was so happy to discover that opera is one of your passions. We need to explore that some more."

"By all means. What are you doing today other than waiting to be paged for a fare? It's such a lovely day. How would you feel about lunch at the del Coronado? It's been too many years since Anton took me there for dinner. If you can see your way clear, would you like me to make a reservation? How about one o'clock?"

"That sounds great. I'll pick you up at noon. It should be a lovely drive down to the port. We'll have some great views from the ferry. The bridge under construction will be of particular interest to me; it is supposed to be operational sometime very soon."

"I'll be ready with bells." He could hear the joy in her voice.

Punctual, as she had become accustomed to in recent days, Julien was waiting for her as she emerged from the Hilton. He was holding the front-seat passenger door open for her. "You look lovely," was his only comment. He gave her a quick peck on her left cheek. Arabella smiled with approval.

"This will be delightful. What a wonderful break from all that "your Honor this" and "your Honor that" and some of the dreadful testimony. I'm thankful to be thinking about something so much more positive and enjoyable. I'm looking forward to the ferry ride. We picked a perfect day to do this."

Julien reached over and lightly touched her gloved left

hand and winked at her. Not in his wildest imagination could he have pictured what was happening when she waved down his cab in front of the courthouse on Monday afternoon. He was beginning to believe that he was at the right place at the right time. "What will we do when the trial is over? Hopefully, it won't go on forever. Of course, the way this old heart feels right now, I don't want it to end," said Julien.

"My dear man, we have plenty of time to figure all of this out. We are both adults, are totally independent, and have means to do almost anything we choose to do. We have a few days to talk about things. I know it's a considerable distance to drive between San Diego and San Luis Obispo. But there are such things as airports; I'm sure you have heard of them? And if we are really serious about it, there might not be any travel involved at all. I'm no longer married to my home in San Luis Obispo, and maybe you'd be willing to change to a larger place here if that needed to be the case. But, as you said last night: "What's the rush?" She hesitated for a moment, "On the other hand, I would like to hear what your intentions are. I'm surprised at myself. Am I the one who is trying to seduce you?"

Julien laughed out loud. "My Thoroughly Modern Millie! I love it. You are a refreshing wind in my sagging sails. You have no idea what these last twenty-four hours have meant to me. When Tatiana died, I thought my life as a man was over. She was everything a man could want in a wife; she was bright, joyful, elegant, interesting, and had an endless joie de vivre. With one stroke, all of it was wiped out. I was terribly lonely and depressed. Sometimes I felt like ending it all. And then, you step up to my cab—and all is changed. Allow me to court you and bring our separate lives together. People talk of love at first sight. It's an epiphany. It's a life-changing event for both of us. Let's enjoy these moments, perhaps leading us to be joint forever as the pronunciation goes." Now Arabella reached over to touch his hand.

"I can do better than that. Let me kiss your cheek. I long to kiss your mouth but don't want us to get killed on our second date. Is that the ferry in front of us? That's a sizable vessel. It looks like you can drive your car right onto the ship."

"Oh yes, my dear. I've got every intention of doing that. You wouldn't want to walk from the pier to the del Coronado in those pretty shoes, would you?"

"Gosh, I hadn't even thought about walking when I got dressed. My mind must have been elsewhere. I probably was mulling over the events of the last day. One doesn't meet a handsome Greek any old time."

Julien beheld her lovingly. "Thanks, I'll tuck that sweet nothing away in my memory box."

As the ferry was moving away from the pier, Julien was all eyes on the new bridge to del Coronado. "This is absolutely fantastic. I'm so glad civilian and military planners could get their acts finally together and agree on the design. It will be a marvel of technology."

"I love the way it gently curves and sweeps out to the island. Beautiful design," said Arabella.

It didn't take all that long before the ferry reached del Coronado. They were among the first cars driving off the ferry. "This surely has changed since I was here with Anton; it was sometime in 1940 or 1941. I know it was definitely before we became embroiled in WWII." Her vision darted everywhere. A few minutes later, Julien had turned his vehicle over to a parking attendant, and they were invited to enter the vestibule. Only seconds went by, and they were seated at a table with a view.

Arabella was perusing the extensive menu and vaguely remembered what Anton ordered for her. When alcoholic beverages were offered, she opted for a virgin frozen Daiquiri. Julien, having to maneuver in heavy traffic on their return to the hotel, wanted lemon water. Both having selected a highly praised seafood salad served on croissants, Julien excused himself, needing to use the facility. Seeing him rush off, Arabella's eyes twinkled.

Julien smiled to himself. His little deception had worked. He was on his way to the floral shoppe within the hotel. He turned toward a busy young florist. "I would like one of these long-stemmed red roses. Please bind it with just a touch of green. I'm about to propose to a very special lady. Make it as pretty as you can."

"Oh, I will. You won't be sorry you came to see me." Within seconds, the rose was de-thorned, trimmed, unnecessary leaves removed, and an attractive green affixed with a lacy white ribbon. "Does this work for you, Sir?"

"Yes, by all means." He paid the young lady and tipped her nicely." He couldn't wait to see the look on Arabella's face. Julien walked up to the table, holding his treasure hidden behind his back. Arabella was reading about the history of the famous hotel and inn. She heard his footsteps as he moved closer and looked up. "It's amazing the people who have stayed here since it opened in 1888. Do you remember what else was so important about 1888 when you studied history? It's the year when Germany had three different Kaisers. Anton talked about that so often."

"Well now, it's my turn. I honor Anton for sure. However, at this very moment, I would like your undivided attention. He went down on his right knee and presented his rose to Arabella. She gasped and then gave him the biggest smile. "My Rosenkavalier, my very own Rosenkavalier!" That was all she dared to say. Just for a split second, the words of the Marschallin from the famous trio in the final act of *Der Rosenkavalier* rang in her ears. Bliss and sadness stole into her heart; tears of remembrance masked her joyful smile as she beheld Julien.

"There wasn't time to get a ring; I didn't believe it to be proper to present you with Tatiana's. But be assured, I'll take care of it pronto, pronto. What do you say? Or did I leave you speechless?"

"That you did. I never thought I would say these words again, but I do accept your proposal. How and when we will marry will be on the back burner for now, although I can't wait for it to happen."

Julien rose from his knee and looked at Arabella. He bent to her gracefully and gave her the kiss she had longed for since the previous evening. Other guests surrounding them in the spectacular dining room of the del Coronado burst into instant applause that went on far too long. Arabella blushed and returned Julien's kiss. At that instant, she was the happiest woman on earth, momentarily forgetting the sadness that had invaded her heart when she first heard Commander Shepherd's words speaking of Juliana Arabella's death.

The luncheon was all that it had promised. The ride back on the ferry presented eye-catching vistas of the San Diego skyline. However, nothing trumped Julien's presentation of the rose and his proposal of marriage. When they walked into the Hilton hand-in-hand, everyone guessed what had taken place. Julien winked at Jesus as they passed the bar.

"You know what to deliver to room #508, Signor, si?"

"Si, Signor Solomika. Coming up right away. Felicidades! Felicidades!"

"Thanks, Jesus," and they stepped in the elevator. They had barely missed Max Weinstein and his entourage walking into the hotel. Julien couldn't wait to embrace Arabella.

He helped Arabella out of her lightweight coat. She handed him her pillbox hat, a souvenir of the Jackie Kennedy era. She went to the restroom and freshened her makeup a bit. She smiled approvingly at her image in the large mirror. *Not too bad for an old lady*, as she winked at herself. *I wonder what he has in mind for tonight? My God, I haven't been with a man in more than twenty-three years*. But she walked out confidently facing her man.

Julien embraced her firmly as a knock was at the door. "That must be our favorite bellhop; Jesus is Johnny-on-the-spot." He took the tray and rewarded the young man according to the way he felt at this very moment. Courtesies were exchanged and they were alone at last. Julien placed her drink into her hand, holding it just for a second. He lifted his own glass toward her and said: "L'Chaim," you taught me something. I love it. Here is to our new life together. May it be a long and happy life; let the outside world not invade the happiness we were allowed to find at last. Here's to Anton and Tatiana; I know we will have their blessings."

Arabella had tears in her eyes; she was deeply touched by Julien's tenderness and sincerity. They enjoyed their Rob Roys and the wonderful selection of petit fours Jesus had prepared for them. "After that luncheon at the del Coronado, I don't feel like a big dinner tonight," said Arabella.

"I totally agree. I'm not big on hefty dinners before I retire for the night. I've gotten into the European routine of having my large meal early in the afternoon. I tend to sleep a lot better when I'm not stuffed to the gills, as some say. By the way, I asked the attendant to put my car into overnight parking. I presume that's OK with you?"

"You read me correctly. I want you to spend these next two days and nights with me. I need to draw on your strength. I'm not sure how I will deal with whatever is to come. I'm afraid there's still a lot of heartache in store for me."

Julien turned on the radio. They were playing "Fascination," one of his favorite waltzes. He took Arabella in his arms and swept her off her feet. "I love to waltz!" was what Julien said. Arabella concurred. "I'd rather dance than eat."

When the sound stilled, they faced each other in Arabella's bedroom. "Don't be afraid; I won't hurt you. Remember, it's been a long time for me too. I might even be out of practice. We must learn to discover each other." He disrobed her gently and she helped him in getting out of his clothes. When they were beholding each other's nakedness, they were doing just that, just holding each other. Julien looked into Arabella's eyes and then gave her a lingering, soft kiss. "I haven't said these words in years but now I must speak them. I love you. Arabella, please be mine!"

Arabella held him firmly in her arms as he aimed to make them both blissfully happy. For just a moment, she hesitated to show her responsiveness toward his lovemaking and then decided to let nature take its course. She was determined to be happy and to make Julien happy for the rest of their days, come what may.

Their first attempts were clearly more rewarding for Julien. Both were looking forward to making their physical closeness mutually enjoyable and satisfying. Arabella and Julien had discovered that there was life after all!

Chapter 27

T_{HE} rays of the low-sitting morning sun awoke Arabella. For a second she didn't realize that she wasn't alone. As she reopened her eyes, she saw Julien still soundly asleep next to her. All she could hear was his breathing. *Why didn't I hear him snoring during the night? Anton always snored when lying on his back.* She stared at his bronzed chest covered with a fleece of curly soft-gray hair. Arabella couldn't resist touching him gently. *I can't believe you are mine.*

"That's so much nicer than some noisy alarm clock telling me it is time to rise and shine." He turned onto his right side, drawing Arabella toward his anxious embrace and kissed her softly. "Good morning. That was a wonderful way to start the day as it was even more wonderful to end the day gone by. What shall we do today, not having to worry about you facing that dismal courtroom procedure? Are you prepared to be called as a witness tomorrow?"

"You did have to spoil my joyous mood by mentioning that dreadful place, didn't you?"

"Sorry, I didn't mean to do that."

"But to answer your question; yes, I'm fully prepared to be on the stand and be questioned and more. I just want this whole affair to be over. It's ruined my life far too long.

"Now, let's plan our day. Could we have breakfast in our room and lay out the day? What did you have in mind when you held me so tightly before?"

"You felt that? I was hoping to start the day with an encore performance of the play we experienced last night, just wanting to make sure you understood the message the author wished to convey."

"Well, aren't you the erudite one. It's like a good book; if it's not worth reading a second time, it wasn't worth reading in the first place." She drew him closer to her, wanting to feel all of him; she couldn't recall how long it had been since she had this urgent desire to be fulfilled by a man. When Julien found his pleasurable release, Arabella moaned loudly, urging him on to bring her to heights of fulfillment.

"Now, wasn't that a memorable second act?" he whispered into her ear.

"Yes, Shakespeare. I can't wait for Acts III, IV, and V. But before we make plans for the evening, let's start with a productive morning. While I enjoy a much-needed shower, will you please call Jesus and have him surprise us with a delectable breakfast. While sipping freshly pressed juices and his delightful Espressos, we'll think of what to do with the rest of this last free day. Does that sound like a plan, Mr. Erudite?"

"I've been called charming, handsome, bright, debonair, suave, and refined, but never in my life have I been called erudite. Must have something to do with that great head of hair I still sport. Must be in the genes; my dad had beautiful hair until the day he died."

"Let me assure you, it's not your handsome head of hair that conveyed that impression to me. It's the way you've conducted yourself from the moment I met you. You truly do not believe I would have fallen in love with you and consider marrying you knowing you for less than one hundred hours just because of a healthy head of hair? Don't get me wrong, your good looks didn't hurt; neither did your performances on the stage of life. But there were the things you would say that let me see what you felt in my presence that allowed me to embrace you wholeheartedly."

She smiled. "Philosophical discussion is closed. I have plans to discuss and places to go. Hold onto your hat, Shakespeare; I'm writing my very own ending to this opus." She drew the shower curtain behind her, fully enjoying the rush of the hot water on her body.

Julien was left with an expectant look on his face, but called Jesus to order their breakfast. He was seriously wondering what Arabella was thinking. He knew what he wanted to do on this new day. Emerging from the shower, Arabella was pummeling her hair. She hated using hairdryers and going to beauty parlors; however, on this day she wanted to make herself as attractive as possible. She was fortunate to have wavy hair always styled and cut to make herself look presentable with little fussing; she had that easy and casual look about her.

"That breakfast looks inviting. Go shave and shower and join me soon. I'll have my first cup of Espresso while sticking my nose into the morning paper." She thought he had a cute butt when she watched him stepping into the shower. He waved at her, not wanting her to glance at him bow side.

✖

"That feels a lot better, although I'll have to stop at my place and change to some clean underwear, sox, and the entire outfit for all intents and purposes. I'm not accustomed to wearing the same rags two days in a row," said Julien emerging from the shower.

"Come, come now. It's not that bad. I certainly wasn't aware of anything odoriferous. Now, sit down, enjoy this breakfast, and let's make plans for the day. There are two things on the top of my list. Our first stop should be the marriage license bureau. Thank God, we no longer are required to have our blood tested. I never knew what that was all about. If we get the license early enough, we might even find a Justice of the Peace or some other likely official to marry us later in the day. It's possible in California."

"Coming back to your earlier question, I happen to know why they did the blood test. They wanted to make sure no one, especially the guy, was a carrier of syphilis or other good things to pass on to the unsuspecting prospective partner. They did away with it earlier this year since so many have kids today without benefit of a marital commitment. And speaking of marital commitment, you are really serious about this, aren't you?"

"Well, Rosenkavalier & Shakespeare, aren't you?"

"I certainly am. Can't wait to get out of here and start the day. What was the second thing on your list?"

"If this all comes to pass, I would like to stop at a dress shop and select an appropriate outfit for the event. Needless to say, I didn't come to this trial expecting to run across and get married to some handsome dog."

"Oh, now I'm an erudite, handsome dog! You are full of compliments this morning." He punched his left hand and laughed out loud. "You didn't ask me what I had in mind? Cartier is right around the corner; I would like to get you a pretty ring, and, as I said before, I want to stop at my place and pack a few things after I change my whole attire, if that is OK with you?"

"Sounds like a plan to me. Did you contact your dispatcher?"

"I did already yesterday. I told her I was off their radar until further notice. It's not the source of my major income. I started driving after Tatiana passed away. Some days I felt like climbing the walls. I needed to get out of that condo and be with people. Driving the cab was my way of saving my sanity. And guess what? I would never have met you!"

"Call the concierge, please. Have the attendant bring up the car from the garage. I'm ready to go." They were on their way within minutes. Jesus, the bellhop, and the concierge gave them their thumbs up and beamed at them. Rarely had they seen anyone as happy as these two on this morning.

"First stop, marriage license bureau, please," whispered Arabella.

"Yes, Ma'am," he gave her a military salute with aplomb. "Haven't done that in a few years, but it's like riding a bike, you never forget." They were lucky to find a convenient parking space near the license bureau. The clerk on hand was charming.

"We would like to take out a marriage license. What do we need to do?"

"Please complete this form. It will only take a few minutes. Both of you will need to sign it. The license fee is fifteen dollars. You may pay with a check or with cash. Which will it be?" Julien reached for his billfold, withdrawing the desired amount.

"What do we need to do to arrange to be married later today? Is that even a possibility?"

"There's an opening with Judge Dulcitt at four o'clock. Could you make that? I'd be more than happy to set it up for you. You can even pay me for the fee. At present, it's still twenty-five dollars."

Julien paid the lady. They were walking out hand-in-hand smiling at each other. "Missions one and two duly accomplished. You have a problem with zipping by my place? I'd feel so much better in a set of fresh underwear." Arabella covered her mouth; she was giggling like a young girl.

It wasn't long and Julien had parked his car in the underground. His parking space bore his name, MG Julien Solomika. Arabella wasn't quite sure what to make of the prefix. They took the elevator to the eighteenth floor. Julien reached for a key in his pocket and opened the elevator. They stepped directly into his penthouse apartment. "Come in, this is my abode."

Arabella looked out at the San Diego harbor and del Coronado in the distance; she could even see Point Loma, barely visible above a bank of low-lying fog. It took her breath away. "Just take a look around and make yourself comfortable while I change my skivvies and the rest." She walked through the great room and admired the completeness of the kitchen. There was absolutely no evidence of disorder or clutter. His plants were well taken care of. She didn't even notice any dust.

As she walked into his bedroom she couldn't help seeing her Greek Adonis standing there in the buff. She walked up to him and hugged him fiercely.

"Let's save it for our wedding night!" said Julien as he quickly slipped into his silk boxers. Arabella couldn't help glancing into his neatly organized closet.

"What's with the fancy uniforms and all that tinsel hanging from the left side of these jackets? Were you a military man? I had no idea. What's that MG in front of your name in the garage?"

"It was Tatiana's idea. She was so proud of my rank. I was a Major General in the Army when I retired in 1958. A year later I lost her."

Arabella noticed the colored photograph of a beautiful woman in an ornate silver frame on the right nightstand. "That was Tatiana before that horrible disease destroyed her. I loved her very much—but you taught me in these last few days that life is for the living. She would have wanted me to find love again." Arabella couldn't help seeing the tears in his eyes. She was inwardly hoping they were tears of joy rather than sadness. She picked up the framed photo and held it for a moment.

"She was beautiful. I hope I can make you as happy in our remaining years."

Julien smiled at her, "You will!"

He gave a quick look into a large mirror. "I'm all changed for the day. You approve of the looks of the man who will be your husband in a matter of hours? I still cannot believe this is happening. I packed a few things in my leather bag. That should do me for the next couple of days. You haven't said anything about my place. You like it? Would you consider trading your house in San Luis Obispo for my pad in San Diego?”

“Actually I was quite taken aback when I walked into your beautiful home. Your views are breathtaking. I can’t get over how neat and orderly everything is. You totally surprised me. We’ll talk about the other matter later. Who keeps this place so nice?”

“Being a military man, I’ve always bordered on being anal in the neatness department. Window washing, toilet cleaning, and dusting I leave to help I’ve coming in twice a month. That works for me.

“I was hoping you would like the place where I hang my hat. If it isn’t big enough for you, we could always move to a larger unit.

“Actually, I have first right of refusal on buying the larger unit next door. The owner is a childless widower, another military man who doesn’t expect to be around for too many more years. We’ve been good friends for a long time and signed said agreement a while ago when I told him I was seriously hoping to find another mate. It must have been in our stars. Who knew?”

“I like a man who looks ahead to the future; little did I know a few days ago that I was meant to be in that future. Now that you are all duded up, I want to find myself something a bit more appropriate for our wedding. Is that OK with you?”

“Yes, by all means. And remember, I need to stop at Cartier and find us some rings; it’s part of the wedding spiel.”

“You mean I’ll get to pick my own rings?”

“If that’s what you want, that’s what it will be.”

Walking by a credenza in the living room, she saw a fairly

recent photograph of Julien resting against a sporty little flying machine. "Is that yours?" she asked.

"Yes, it is one of my hobbies. I love to hop on it and just take off for the day and go some place totally frivolous. There are so many places nearby that are easily accessible with my Piper Colt. Maybe one of these days, we head up to San Francisco and take in *Arabella* at the War Memorial Opera House. How does that sound to you?"

"It sounds divine!"

Standing by the parked car, Arabella looked once again at the sign, and then couldn't help seeing the content of his large trunk as he was putting in his leather satchel, ready to push down the lid.

"What's in that canister? Do you always have it with you."

"It's almost mandatory for a cab to carry a spare canister of fuel. One never knows when one might need to use it." She nodded in agreement and let Julien help her into the car.

The concierge had advised Arabella of an elegant shoppe where she would find what she was looking for. She told Julien about *Extravaganza,* and he knew exactly where it was located.

"May we stop there next? If they have what I want, it won't take me long. I've never been known to dillydally around."

"It's just after noon; you can take all the time you need. But do remember my last stop before we head to City Hall."

Extravaganza was what Arabella had been searching for. She was greeted courteously and shown to a dressing room. "I would like something in a lace-ribbon in three-quarter length. Nothing really dark or in pastel shades. And, of course, nothing stark white. It's the second time around, and I must consider my age."

"No problem, Ma'am; I believe I know what you are searching for. I believe you take a size ten petite; did I guess correctly?"

"You certainly have. Is the one in very pale taupe available in my size?"

"I believe we have it in our stock area. Let me check. That color suits you perfectly. It compliments the shade of your hair."

Walking by Julien, she held up the dress for his approval. He winked at her and gave her a thumbs-up. "Here we are Ma'am; was this what you had in mind? You might want to try it on before you say 'no.' That particular dress always looks better on than shown on a hanger."

"I actually like it, even on the hanger. But, of course, I want my husband-to-be to put his stamp of approval on it. It's not like having to preclude him from viewing the bridal dress at an inopportune moment. We are way past that sort of nonsense and superstition. Let me slip it on. It's perfect as far as I'm concerned, but I want him to see it on me."

"What do you think, Shakespeare? You think it will work in Acts III, IV, and V?"

"Lord Dudley approves, Madame," he bowed from his waist. Arabella and the clerk couldn't help laughing.

"Now, all I need is a pair of heels, not too high, that will compliment the dress. My purse and mink wrap will work just fine with it." Ten minutes later they were on their way to Cartier.

"We need two wedding bands, relatively simple. Neither one of us wants anything really wide or fancy."

"These Lohengrin bands are always popular with your generation." The guy had sized them up when they walked into the emporium of glitz and glamor. Arabella and Julien nodded with approval. "It's just a question of sizing them and that is done in a matter of minutes. We always have several goldsmiths on duty. What else may I show you?" Arabella opted to speak first.

"Since you insist on buying me an engagement ring and having me select it, I'll share my preferences with you. Personally, I view the whole thing as superfluous at this point in our lives. But I know men. I do not want another diamond; perhaps a small emerald or sapphire would suit me perfectly."

"That's helpful," said the elegantly attired gentleman behind the counter. Let me show you what we have. Is there a particular cut you would prefer, Madam?"

"I like an emerald cut; it suits the length of my fingers." She looked down at a plethora of sapphire rings set in platinum or white gold. The choice was difficult. Eventually, she settled on one that appeared to be slightly larger than one carat. I believe I would like to see what this one looks like on my hand." "Mr. Cartier" was astute enough, deftly slipping off the price tag before he slid the ring on Arabella's left hand and giving Julien a quick wink while she was still looking at other rings.

"This one is perfect, if you insist. I love the shape and the color. It will go perfectly with earrings I've had for years." Julien signaled his approval. "I'll have these rings sized for you promptly. Would you care for tea or Espresso? It's right over there at our minibar. Please make yourself comfortable, Ma'am. I can help you at this register, Sir." Arabella thought: *True to form. Get me out of the way and hit him up for the dough.*

"Whereto for lunch?" asked Julien. "Actually, I'm starved. That was quite a tour de force."

"Surprise me; you know this city inside and out."

"There's a charming little French bistro not very far from

here. I've never ordered anything there I didn't enjoy. You'll like it."

Ten minutes later, they were seated in a semi-dark, secluded corner, very intimate and charming. Lots of deep reds on the upholstered chairs and in the background. Arabella thought of the New Year's Eve scene at the nightclub in Moscow in *Dr. Zhivago*; he remembered Nancy Wilson's incomparable rendition of "Guess Who I Saw Today?"

She reached out to touch his hands. "I love it; it's utterly charming. The menu looks great. I'll have some escargot and the French dip. It sounds divine. What'll you have? Any favorites?" She waved her hand toward Julien's face, casting brilliant flashes of deep blue into his laughing eyes. The waiter couldn't help smiling.

"I'll go for the oysters Rockefeller and a petite filet, medium rare. That ought to sustain me through this exiting afternoon."

"Exciting? How about life changing?" He had ordered two glasses of Pinot Noir. Julien lifted his crystal goblet and touched Arabella's. With one voice they toasted each other, "L'Chaim!" That was all that needed to be said.

※

They arrived in a timely fashion at the courthouse and were ushered into Judge Dulcitt's office by his clerk. One might have expected them to be somewhat nervous, had one known the circumstances under which they met and the unbelievable rapidity of reaching this very moment. But they weren't nervous at all. Excited, yes, but not nervous or filled with trepidation.

Judge Dulcitt greeted them by name; the license documents

had been presented to him just before they arrived. "Please stand in front of me." As he began to recite their marriage vows, both Arabella and Julien had tears in their eyes when they were listening to the all-too-well-known

phrases: "...to have and to hold from this day forward, for better, for worse, for richer, for poorer, in sickness and in health, to love and to cherish, till death do us part."

They placed the rings on each other's hands and joyfully kissed when Judge Dulcitt pronounced them husband and wife. It was close to sunset when they emerged from City Hall.

"Hilton, Southwest, please." She was catching her breath. "Thank you for being there, when I needed you the most. Thank you for falling in love with me and not being afraid to show it. Make sure you arrange for overnight parking. I've no intentions of sharing you with anyone else on this night. Now, you are really mine. Catch Jesus's eye as we glide by on our way to the lift. Rob Roys and petit fours are all I need. I'll let you handle the sex. My, my! I never thought I would say that word."

Julien cracked up as he jumped out of the car wanting to help Arabella alight from her chariot. "Lord Dudley, at your service." He extended his right hand toward hers. She looked stunning in her new dress highlighted by the dark mink wrap. All she needed was a tiara, but then, she was his queen, tiara or no tiara.

He tipped the attendant and gave the necessary instructions where to park the car. Julien walked his queen into the Hilton. In years past, he would have looked resplendent in one of his dress uniforms; today he looked handsome in his three-piece, deep-blue serge Kuppenheimer suit. Who would have wanted to cover his gorgeous gray hair with a top hat or some military cap?

"Lord and Lady Dudley" made it safely to room #508; there were loud cheers and whistles all over the lobby. "We've done it!" said Julien as he took Arabella firmly into his arms. She set the mink wrap on one of the other chairs and took a seat. "Now, I'm ready for that Rob Roy. The petit fours, I could skip. Perhaps I'll have them later with a nightcap. That lunch was sumptuous and more like a dinner. The escargot were divine." She heard a soft knock on the door.

"Please, answer the door and be generous with that boy. He's so sweet."

Ferdi set the drinks and petit fours on the cocktail table. "Congratulations, Madam, congratulations, Sir. We are all rooting for you." Thank you, Ferdi. You have a good evening. Perhaps we'll call for another round later. Shall see how these two old fogies shall fare."

Ferdi had barely closed the door behind him, when Arabella let him have it. "Who do you call an old fogy? I'm not even sixty years old and you are barely there. If it wasn't for these spectacular Rob Roys, I'd have you out of those fancy duds and in bed. I'll show you, old fogy! You awakened a sleeping dragon last night and this morning. You just wait until I get you close to me again!"

Arabella lifted her Rob Roy toward Julien. "L'Chaim!" There was nothing else to say or tell.

Chapter 28

AT last the dreaded Friday morning had arrived. Arabella Davos Knecht Solomika had chosen to enter the courthouse incognito and seated herself in her lonely back row of the courtroom. Again she was cloaked in her black disguise. Julien let her walk in by herself as she had wished. He parked his Mercedes in the underground garage and took the elevator up to the first floor. He chose to seat himself surrounded by numerous spectators. Publicity with reference to Judge Horowitz's alleged heart attack and the name of the defendant had caught the public's attention. There was hardly a free seat in the courtroom.

Previous witnesses were gathered in the back section of the courtroom on the opposite side from where Arabella elected to sit. Commander Shepherd nodded a welcome toward Sylvia; he was pleased she had chosen to be with Homer on this day. Howard recalled the sad story Homer shared with him the day he reported on the details of the coroner's findings. He had never seen Homer Elias Annapolis as sad as he was on that day.

Just before the opening of today's session, another intriguing female figure entered the courtroom. Her clothes were elegant in style but subdued in tone. She was wearing a rakish cloche and very dark sunglasses. She elected to keep shadowing her eyes even while seated inside.

Veronica had insisted on being present. Her ice-blue Chanel suit, daring hat, and noisily clicking heels had caught everyone's attention when she entered Court.

The door to the judge's chamber opened and Judge Horowitz emerged. Bailiff Butler took to the floor.

"Please rise. The Court of the Ninth Judicial Circuit, Criminal Division, is now in session, the Honorable Judge Nathaniel Horowitz presiding."

Judge Horowitz addressed the Court: "Ladies and gentlemen of the Jury, you are still under oath.

"Madame Prosecutor, please call your next witness."

"Thank you, your Honor. I call to the stand Morris Finkelstein."

Mr. Finkelstein walked to the front of the courtroom.

"Will the witness please remain standing to be sworn in by the bailiff?"

Bailiff Butler addressed Mr. Finkelstein. "Please raise your right hand. Do you swear to tell the truth, the whole truth, and nothing but the truth?" Morris Finkelstein placed his right hand hesitatingly on the Bible. He knew it was the Bible and not the New Testament.

"I do," said Mr. Finkelstein, who then walked to the witness stand and sat down.

Hermione Grand approached the witness. Well rested after the two-day recess, Ms. Grand approached the man in her inimitable stance, looking him squarely into his eyes.

"Please state your full name."

"My name is Morris Abraham Finkelstein. I'm forensic medical advisor to Coroner Fortran."

"Do you have a doctoral degree?"

"Yes, Madam Prosecutor. I received my forensic medical degree at Duke University in 1958."

"Dr. Finkelstein, please tell this court in which capacity you functioned relative to the defendant."

"After Coroner Fortran examined the contents of a pouch carried by the alleged victim when she was brought to the mortuary on September 24, 1968, he requested my consultation relative to a typed note found in said pouch. After careful examination of the paper, I was able to confirm the presence of two sets of fingerprints. One set of prints belonged to the alleged victim; the other fingerprints were those of an undetermined individual.

My services were called upon for a second time on Monday, September 30, 1968. Commander Shepherd had secured a sample of the defendant's fingerprints during his visit to the Alvis estate in San Luis Obispo on Friday, September 27, 1968. Dr. Fortran requested comparison studies of these two pieces of evidence."

"Objection," spoke Max Weinstein.

"On what grounds do you object, Mr. Weinstein?" asked Judge Horowitz.

"The second piece of evidence in question was obtained deceptively by Commander Shepherd during his second interrogation at the Alvis estate on September 27, 1968."

"Not true! Mr. Horatio Alvis III provided the document in question totally voluntarily without any coercion by Commander Shepherd. The defendant was completely surprised by the Commander's appreciation of the classic old Remington Rand in his office and was most anxious to demonstrate its usefulness by typing that silly test sentence: "The quick brown fox jumped over the lazy dog." He was delighted to hand the product to the Commander," stated Hermione Grand for the prosecution.

Judge Horowitz got the attention of both attorneys. "Counsel, approach the bench, please.

Mr. Weinstein, in view of Ms. Grand's description of what took place at the Alvis estate on September 27, 1968, I'm inclined to overrule. If you so desire, you may wish to recall Commander Shepherd to the stand, Mr. Weinstein."

"I accept your ruling, your Honor," replied Max Weinstein for the defense.

"The witness may continue," said Judge Horowitz.

Dr. Finkelstein made eye contact with the prosecutor. "Fingerprints on paper are not easily read. However, when I examined the full sheet of paper in question, excellent prints were readable and clearly originated with a single individual. I compared these to some we lifted off that small note in the alleged victim's pouch. They are a perfect match; there's absolutely no doubt in my head that both pieces of paper were handled by one and the same person. Furthermore, both pieces were typed on the same typewriter and carry identical watermarks. There wasn't much of the watermark on the little note in the pouch but enough to corroborate that they were from an identical source. Without question, both notes were typed and handled by the defendant, Mr. Horatio Alvis III."

Momentarily, the hush in the courtroom was broken. The

darkly cloaked figure in the back row was sobbing uncontrollably; her actions were condoned by Judge Horowitz. Veronica's outburst was far more offensive.

"You stupid man; how could you do such an idiotic thing?" she voiced not too softly while glaring at her husband, the defendant.

Judge Horowitz resorted to the use of his gavel; he slammed it into the bench as hard as he was capable of doing. "Order in the court!" There was no *please*. Veronica had challenged him once too often.

"There will not be further offensive voicings in this Court without consequences. Do you read me, Madam?"

He had Veronica's full attention.

"You have anything to add to your statements?" asked the prosecutor of Dr. Finkelstein, still sitting at the witness stand.

"No. I believe I have stated all that is pertinent to your questions."

Judge Horowitz looked at Dr. Finkelstein: "The defense may cross-examine the witness."

"Defense has no other questions for this witness. Thank you, your Honor," said Max Weinstein.

"You may step down," said Judge Horowitz to the witness.

"Prosecution, you may call your next witness."

"Thank you, your Honor. I call to the stand Arabella Davos Knecht."

The darkly cloaked figure arose in the back of the courtroom and walked gracefully to the front.

"Will the witness please remain standing to be sworn in by the bailiff?"

Bailiff Butler stared at the heavily disguised figure standing before him. He wasn't quite certain how to deal with this witness. "Please raise your right hand. Do you swear to tell the truth, the whole truth, and nothing but the truth?" Arabella literally clutched the Bible presented to her by the bailiff.

"I do," said Arabella, who then walked to the witness stand and sat down.

Hermione Grand approached this witness with trepidation; she knew who she was and was anxious to learn what she would have to say.

"Please state your full name."

"My name is Arabella Davos Knecht Solomika." Hermione Grand was startled by the mention of the last surname." She looked at the witness in a quizzical manner.

"Madam, I must ask you to remove your veil. The Court and I must be able to discern your full face; even individuals wearing facial coverings for religious reasons must reveal substantial portions of their faces during testimony given in Court."

Arabella responded to the prosecutor's request by removing her cloche and the attached veil. Hermione Grand wondered why a woman as beautiful as Arabella would resort to such a severe disguise.

"My records show you as Mrs. Arabella Davos Knecht; is there an error in our data?"

"No, Madam Prosecutor, there isn't. I was married to Major General Julien Solomika on January 17, 1969."

"Oh, goodness. You are a new bride. Congratulations! Sorry to interrupt your honeymoon. But may we proceed with our task at hand? Please tell us how you know Mr. Horatio Alvis III and what your connection is to the defendant."

"Mr. Alvis and I were young when we met at a dance in 1929. It was shortly before the financial crash. While our parents were comfortable, they would never have been called rich. I suppose, Mr. Alvis was used to affluence to a larger degree than was I. His father was a member of the Morro Bay Yacht Club and kept a small yacht at the place. I've always been in love with sailing and the sea. I'm sure my love for sailing was what prompted Mr. Alvis to acquire the boat in 1930. He eventually kept it at the club.

"When it was time to name the vessel, he chose to name it *Arabella*. I gather, he was in love with me. I never dreamt of having a boat carry my name. He often whispered to me that he loved the sound of it. By the summer of 1932, I had become a pretty good sailor under the tutelage of Horatio. It was in the fall of that year that I received a phone call from Mr. Alvis, telling me that our affair had run its course. He had met the woman he wished to marry." Arabella took a deep breath.

"Madam Prosecutor, would it be possible for me to have some water. My throat is so dry. Thank you."

The Bailiff retrieved a bottle of water from a case near his desk, setting it and a plastic glass in front of Arabella. "Here you are, Madam. Would you like me to open that bottle for you?"

"Thank you, that is kind of you," smiled Arabella.

"May we proceed with your testimony? Madam," spoke Ms. Grand.

"At first I was terribly hurt, but like all jilted, young, first lovers, I moved on with my life. I was thankful for the love of my parents and for the thoughtfulness of close friends. I was surprised to receive a note from Horatio in early January of 1934, asking me to meet him at the Morro Bay Yacht Club for dinner. At first I was hesitant but then I agreed to meet with him when he called me a few days later. My mother tried to dissuade me but I did it anyway. He wined and dined me and told me of his unhappy marriage. He called his wife a 'rich-bitch ice block,' which took me by total surprise. He told me his wife was pregnant with their first child, and that Veronica had absolutely nothing to do with him. I wasn't quite certain how to respond to his tales of woe. Had I been more astute, I would have known where his story was leading.

"It was a surprisingly mild evening for January, and he asked me to go for a constitutional after the sumptuous meal at the club. I don't know how, but soon we were both facing the *Arabella*. He asked me if I was wanting to take her for a short sail. Not to worry, there were warm jackets stored in the hull. Like a fool, I fell for his overtures. Once out of the harbor, he dropped anchor and proceeded to sweet talk me into joining him for a nightcap below deck. Next thing I knew, he had succeeded in ripping off my clothes, dropped his pants, and literally raped me. I screamed loudly but no one heard me."

Arabella took another sip of water. There were tears in her eyes and hate and disgust written all over her face as she stared at the defendant. Veronica was clasping her mouth.

Sylvia reached for Homer's hand. "Please hold me tight. I feel the sorrow of Arabella Knecht in my every bone. I cannot imagine what is going through that woman's mind."

"Would you like to take a break, Mrs. Solomika?" asked Hermione Grand.

"No, not really. Now that you have me up here, I might as well get done with it. You haven't heard half of what is yet to come.

"He sailed the cutter back to its slip and carried me, feeling like a rag doll, back to his car. At least he didn't dump me.

We drove back to my parents' home in San Luis Obispo and hardly spoke a word. The man had the nerve to ask me to see him again in days to come. He hadn't meant to assault me and claimed he was still madly in love with me. That was the last time I saw Horatio Alvis III until this week when he walked into this courtroom.

"A month after the episode at the yacht club, I knew I was with child. I made up my mind not to confront my parents with my problems since my father was experiencing serious health issues. I managed to find myself a job, working at some low-life motel in South Central LA. It was there that Juliana Arabella was born on October 23, 1934. She was a beautiful child and my pride and joy. I was able to have her with me during those trying times at working at the motel.

"Juliana Arabella was two years old when I met Anton Knecht, who was ten years older than I. We fell in love and the kind man married me within months after meeting us. He loved Juliana and insisted on adopting her. It was only then that my parents learned of Juliana's existence. Anton and I decided not to break their hearts; to my parents and the rest of the world, Anton was a widower with a young child. Juliana loved Anton and he in turn adored her. When she was ten years old, we shared with her that Anton was not her biological father; we never let her know who had fathered her.

"My father died in early 1942 and I frequently looked after my mother, who opted to stay in her house in San Luis Obispo. Anton had built us a beautiful home in Glendale. He was in the banking business and was known as a financial wizard. When he died in 1946, he left my child and me well provided for. I chose to remain in my Glendale home until my mother passed away."

Arabella needed to take another sip of water. She decided there was nothing else to add to her story. When she didn't continue speaking, Hermione Grand came to her rescue.

"Does this conclude your testimony, Mrs. Solomika?"

"Yes, I believe I said all that needed to be said."

Judge Horowitz looked at Arabella. "The defense may cross-examine the witness."

"Defense has no questions for this witness at this time. I reserve the right to recall her later. Thank you, your Honor," said Max Weinstein.

"You may step down," said Judge Horowitz to the witness.

Arabella rose from the witness stand slowly. She returned the cloche and veil to her head and gained her footing as she stepped down. She couldn't avoid seeing Horatio and Veronica Alvis and was thankful that the veil precluded making eye contact with the defendant and his wife.

Approaching the back of the courtroom, she noticed the woman seated next to the man who had been the first witness for the prosecution on day one of the trial. She remembered vaguely that the man had something to do with the Old Lighthouse at Point Loma. Why was this woman crying out her eyes? *Did she know something that had not been shared before the Court?*

Just then Judge Horowitz used his gavel. "Court is recessed for lunch until two o'clock."

Bailiff Butler asked all to rise as Judge Horowitz headed for his chambers. Continuing her walk up the aisle, Arabella gestured to Julien that she wanted him to join her as she felt the need for some fresh air and a change of venue.

"Thank God, that's behind me. I'm hoping Weinstein isn't making good on his promise to recall me," she said softly to Julien.

"You did well up there. That had to be pretty rough to tell your story to the world. Some of it, you hadn't shared with me. I wasn't even aware of the fact that Horatio was Juliana's father. That scumbag, raping you! I was under the impression that Anton was her father."

"For all intents and purposes, he was. He loved her like his own and took great care of her and me. We would never have been able to live and do as we did if it hadn't been for that loving man. Do you know who that woman is, sitting next to that handsome old man with that crop of snow-white hair? I believe he's the one who found the cutter on the beach and discovered Juliana's body."

"I don't. I assume it's the man's wife. Age-wise they fit together."

"Well, maybe when this is all behind us, I would like to speak to her. She seems to be terribly upset by what she heard this morning. But, let's give it a rest for now. I need some air and a good lunch. We can walk to that little French bistro you took me to yesterday. I loved the ambiance and the food, and—I could use the walk."

"Have the oysters Rockefeller and the petite filet; you'll love it. It's quick and it will give you a lift. I better not order any wine, especially if they recall you. I think I'll go for the French dip; that looked good."

"Now that we have all that settled, we'll make it quick and easy for the garçon de café." She swallowed for a moment. "I would have loved to have seen the expression on Veronica's face when I related what that man of hers did to me. I noticed the courtroom artist busily sketching her and me. It will be interesting to see those impressions in print. There I go again, being the one who wanted a change of subject matter. You must forgive me; it does weigh heavily on my mind. I promise, no other comments during lunch. One more thing, I was terribly proud to say that I'm Mrs. Solomika. And speaking of honeymoon, we haven't even had time to think about that. Give it some serious thought. How about two weeks in Hawaii? I know just the spot. Have you been there?"

"Yes, but not under the best of circumstances. I'd love to discover what it is all about in peace time."

Chapter 29

THEY enjoyed their lunch. Time had flown by all too quickly, and they were back on their way to the courthouse. Soon all were seated again in their preferred or designated areas in the courtroom. Judge Horowitz emerged from his chambers.

Bailiff Butler sprung into action. "Please rise. The Honorable Judge Nathaniel Horowitz presiding."

Judge Horowitz addressed the Court: "Ladies and gentlemen of the Jury, you are still under oath.

"Madame Prosecutor, please call your next witness."

"Thank you, your Honor. The prosecution rests."

"Mr. Weinstein, are you ready with the defense?" asked Judge Horowitz.

"Yes, your Honor. I am calling my one and only witness, the defendant Horatio Alvis III.

Horatio got up and walked toward the witness stand.

"Will the witness please remain standing to be sworn in by the bailiff?"

Bailiff Butler addressed Mr. Alvis. "Please raise your right hand. Do you swear to tell the truth, the whole truth, and nothing but the truth?" Every time the word truth was stated, Horatio Alvis appeared to wince and shrink in height. He barely made contact with the Bible when the bailiff extended it to him.

"I do," said Horatio Alvis, who then stepped into the witness stand and sat down.

Hermione Grand had taken her seat. Her vision was glued on the witness and his counsel. An almost eerie silence had fallen over the courtroom. After Arabella Solomika's testimony, spectators and interested parties were full of anticipation of the presentation by the next witness. Many were taken by total surprise that the defendant had agreed to testify on his own behalf.

Max Weinstein stepped close to the witness box.

"Mr. Alvis, please tell the Court your side of the equation. Let me remind you that you are under oath and pledged to tell the truth and nothing but the truth. Please proceed."

"I was born into a solid middle class family in 1907. At the time of my birth, my parents lived in Bakersfield, California. I remained an only child. My father was in academia and took a position at California Polytechnic State University, San Luis Obispo, in 1922. It was a difficult time for me; I had to leave all my friends behind, and making new friends at a new high school was hard for me, especially since I started school halfway into the fall term. Eventually, I adjusted and made the best of a difficult situation.

"Being an only child, my mother had a tendency to indulge me. My father was a true taskmaster and made undue demands on my intellectual abilities. He expected me to follow in his footsteps, although I never showed much promise and was an extreme disappointment to him when I declined to pursue any studies beyond high school. I fell in love with anything that moved: trains, boats, cars—you name it.

"After high school I found a job with a car dealership. Although totally distraught with my occupational choices, we found a common ground by liking sailing. My father was pleased that I enjoyed our regular outings on the sailboat he kept at the Morro Bay Yacht Club. Dad was an excellent sailor, having learned his skills during his years of studying in England.

"As Mrs. Solomika testified, we met at a dance in San Luis Obispo in 1929; she was eighteen and I was twenty-two years old. It was love at first sight. I pursued her vigorously although she conveyed to me early on in our relationship that she was a *good girl* and unwilling to jump into the sack with a half-baked car salesman. For Arabella, it was marriage or nothing at all. Not making a lot of money as a starting salesman in the automobile business and not expecting any sort of handout from my parents, I couldn't afford to get married. My father wanted me to have my own boat and encouraged me to use some of my savings and buy a small vessel. I did so in 1930. He was willing to pay for the mooring slip and my membership in the club. All I had to offer Arabella were rides on my small sailboat.

"My monetary problems were solved when I met Veronica in 1932. I broke off my relationship with Arabella Davos quite suddenly. Veronica was not only a stunner, but she came from a well-heeled, prominent family. She oozed affluence, making things possible for me I had never dreamt of. Best yet, I had found sexual contentment in the arms of Veronica Hofmeister. We were married a year later and lived in a charming little apartment in Sacramento. In October of 1933, I learned from

Veronica that we would be having a child more likely than not no later than August of 1934.

"Veronica's father died suddenly during his attempt at being reelected to the governorship. We and Veronica's mother elected to move back to San Luis Obispo. Her mother reclaimed the familial estate of her deceased parents, and we found convenient and adequate housing in town. I did some odd jobs here and there but was mostly a kept man, so to speak. While at first I was thrilled to learn that I could possibly have produced Alvis IV, frustration set in when Veronica refused my marital rights. After her first trimester she decided to become celibate. Needless to say, that didn't set well with my twenty-seven-year-old hormone pool.

"It was early in 1934 that I wrote the letter to Arabella, begging her to meet with me. I dined with her at the Morro Bay Yacht Club and shared my heartache. And yes, I did refer to my wife as the 'rich-bitch ice block.' What happened next, I'm not proud of. When I suggested the boat ride on the *Arabella*, I had no intentions of assaulting Ms. Davos. I knew Arabella would not willingly have me. I don't know what possessed me. I was driven by my physical needs to possess her on that fateful evening. And yes, I took her forcefully. I did rape her.

"I regret what I did; what I regret the most is the fact that we never again crossed paths until we met in this court-room. Even more so, I'm truly sorry never to have known that Arabella bore me a daughter. I hate to confess my marriage to Veronica has been one of convenience and being endowed with limitless financial security but not one founded on enduring love."

Veronica screamed, "You goddamn bastard."

Judge Horowitz banged his gavel with anger and fury. "Madam, one more outburst from you and I will have you expelled from the proceedings. Do you understand me? I will not tolerate your behavior in my courtroom." Veronica covered her ears and put her head down on the table. She didn't care to hear or see anymore of her husband's damning testimony.

"Mr. Weinstein, advise your client to continue with his testimony," said Judge Horowitz.

"Our son, Horatio Alvis IV, met Juliana Knecht while they both attended medical school, he in pursuit of a degree in internal medicine, Ms. Knecht in pharmacology. According to our son, theirs was strictly a platonic relationship. They dined out together on occasion, saw plays, attended concerts, and in time Junior discovered that Ms. Knecht shared his love for sailing. He taught her to sail the *Arabella*. As his social interests waned, he gave her access to the boat and allowed her to sail it on her own. There were times when I wondered if our son was gay. However, that is not the case. Perhaps he takes after his mother rather than myself. I've been accused numerous times of being a ladies' man.

"Two years ago, in November, I met our son for lunch at the yacht club when Ms. Knecht spotted Horatio Jr. and walked over to say 'hello.' She was meeting a girlfriend for lunch. After Junior made the introductions, we chatted for a while. She seemed to enjoy the conversation and winked at me when her luncheon companion arrived. Her friend was totally shy, perhaps due to her appearance. I believe she was a burn victim and had seen much plastic surgery on her face. I took that casual wink by Ms. Knecht as an invitation to the dance. I asked Junior for her telephone number. He questioned the appropriateness of my contacting Ms. Knecht. I assured him that it would be nice for me to have a friendly face across from me in a restaurant once in awhile.

"The first time Ms. Knecht and I met alone, it was evident that she was not disinclined to be seen with a graying gentleman. We met almost weekly over a glass of wine and delightful dinners. Our tête-à-tête meals were a pleasant diversion and followup to the dreaded encounters with my friend, Ernest, whom I see regularly each weekend. His progression with dementia was depressing. In time, I invited Ms. Knecht to join me on the *Horatio III*, the yacht my wife had bought for me. One thing led to another and eventually Ms. Knecht enjoyed being romanced and sexually attended to by a mature man.

"In June of last year, my lover informed me that she was pregnant. There was no question that I was the father of the unborn child since I was the only man she saw on a regular basis. I contemplated divorcing Veronica and marrying the young woman. Veronica wouldn't hear of it. As far as Ms. Knecht was concerned, abortion was totally out of the question.

"In early September, Juliana confronted me with something that I found utterly disturbing.

She had visited her mother, and in the evening they had perused a large box holding all sorts of photos dating back over the years. Among them was a photo of me when I was twenty-four years old. Juliana continued to question her mother as to the identity of the man in the photo, but was given only vague answers. She speculated that perhaps the photo depicted the father whom she had never known. With that seed planted, she insisted that both she and I have a blood analysis done. She received the results on Wednesday, September 18, 1968. When she called me, she was dissolved in tears and wanted to see me that evening.

"We met on my yacht. Before I could even take her into my arms, she lost it: 'Not only are you my father but also the father of this child I'm carrying. How are you seeing yourself dealing with our situation? I realize it isn't your fault that I fell in love with an unknown man who happens to be my father. Perhaps I should have taken you up on the offer to abort this child when you asked me weeks ago. It is too late now.'

"I tried to console her and assured her I would do some investigating and that we would meet the next night on the yacht. I was hoping to have answers for her. I contacted the offices of a Dr. Harm in South Central LA. In my search, I learned that he performed advanced-term abortions for a sizable amount of money. Yes, I did type that infamous note on my typewriter and included the information of the abortion clinic. One thousand dollars were in the same envelope that held the typed note. We met only briefly that evening since both of us believed we were being observed. I handed her the envelope and urged her strongly to pursue this only way out of our dilemma. We didn't kiss but simply walked away from each other. It was the last time I saw Juliana. It is the truth and nothing but the truth so help me God!"

Horatio Alvis III was sobbing as he bent down his head, shutting out all eyes glaring at him.

Max Weinstein was stunned, as were all sitting in the courtroom. "Mr. Alvis, does this conclude your testimony?"

"Yes," was barely audible as he tried to clear his throat.

Judge Horowitz spoke: "Did I understand you to say earlier that the defendant was the only witness you wished to present?"

"Yes, your Honor, that is what I said."

"In that case, I propose that you and Ms. Grand make your closing statements to the Jury."

As the last of the judge's words faded away, a woman arose among the spectators and approached Ms. Grand. "I was not summoned by either you or the defense to testify. However, I believe I have information that might have significant impact on the outcome of this trial. I wish to testify at this point."

Hermione Grand secured the attention of Judge Horowitz. "Your Honor, may we approach the bench?"

"Please do, Madam Prosecutor, Mr. Weinstein."

"The young woman standing by my desk has just approached me wishing to testify. She claims to have important information that may ultimately determine the outcome of this trial."

"What is your disposition, Mr. Weinstein?"

"If you and Ms. Grand would want to pursue this matter, I have no objections, your Honor. After the testimony of the defendant, nothing would surprise me, your Honor."

"Bailiff Butler, please swear in the witness."

Bailiff Butler confronted the witness. "Please raise your right hand. Do you swear to tell the truth, the whole truth, and nothing but the truth?" The witness was void of all facial expression; she acted as if she were surrounded by a thick fog. Her hands shook as she touched the Bible presented to her by Bailiff Butler.

"I do," she whispered, then stepped into the witness stand and sat down. Hermione Grand advised the witness to remove her dark glasses and to speak more clearly, allowing the recorder to write down what she said.

All eyes in the courtroom were on the strange figure having stepped forward. Only Arabella knew who she was. Sylvia nudged Homer gently with her right elbow. "Do you have any idea what this is all about? Isn't it odd that someone would step forward this late in the trial? From what I've learned today, I want this Alvis guy to get his comeuppance. He's as guilty as they come. That poor woman, what she must have suffered for all these months since you first discovered that boat at our shores." Homer touched his lips with his right index finger, signaling for Sylvia to stop whispering.

Judge Horowitz was taking a particular interest in the person he presumed to be the last witness for the day.

"Please state your full name, Ma'am," said Judge Horowitz.

"My name is Ulrike Marianne Hammer."

Prosecutor Grand instructed the witness.

"Please tell the Court how you know the defendant and what important information you believe to hold in your possession. Let me remind you, you are testifying under oath. Please proceed."

"First of all, I do not know the defendant, I only know of him. The person I did know was Juliana A. D. Knecht, my closest friend since we sat next to each other in junior high. We studied pharmacology at the same university and have remained friends all through the years. I'm in possession of two letters that were written by Juliana before she disappeared. I received these letters in my mail on September 24, 1968; that is, a so-called cover letter was postmarked in Morro Bay and dated September 20, 1968. Allow me to read you the content of the cover letter."

Dearest Ulrike,

I'm at the Morro Bay Yacht Club where I met my gentleman friend earlier. He left an envelope with me which I'm not supposed to open until I am alone. The seas are a bit choppy; nevertheless, I intend to go out for a boat ride. I've sailed that craft in all sorts of weather and am looking forward to the challenge. There are too many question marks in my life these days, and I believe you are the only one I can trust with my unusual request. There might come a time when the evening news will be of special interest to you. Read the enclosed letter *only* under certain circumstances. You will know when to do so. Use this instrument wisely.

Much love,

Your friend Juliana

"The letter to which Juliana makes reference, I have not opened but intend to at this very moment. It is my sincere hope the many questions held in this room will find the answers in what I am about to read."

She asked Bailiff Butler for a letter opener and proceeded slowly, since she had no way of explaining the thickness of the letter. When she reached into the opened envelope, several one-hundred-dollar bills spilled to the floor. She retrieved them, placing the money on the desk in front of her. When taking out the folded letter, several more bills spilled on the desk. Ulrike did not bother to count them. She glanced down at Juliana's familiar handwriting and began to read.

Dearest Ulrike,

By the time you read this letter, I'll be long gone and hopefully safely held in the arms of our Lord. I'm fully aware of the church's position on suicide, and yet, I firmly believe in the existence of a loving and forgiving God who shall welcome this sinner. Please do not cry at my revelations. What I am about to do is in the best interest of all who will be affected by my decision to end my life.

When I discovered weeks ago that I was pregnant with Horatio's child, I resolved to have his boy or girl and raise the child on my own, knowing fully that Veronica would never agree to a divorce. I would have loved to be married to Horatio, but that wasn't meant to be. Horatio was willing to pay for an abortion when I first let him know that I was pregnant. I couldn't do it.

You probably believe things cannot get any worse. Two weeks ago or so, spending an evening with my mother, I saw a photo, among many she apparently held dear, that looked an awful lot like Horatio when he was in his twenties. When I questioned her as to the identity of that man, she gave me nothing but vague answers. Discussing my find with Horatio, I didn't gain any further knowledge. It was my instinct that led me to pursue blood studies involving both of us. I received the lab results two days ago.

Don't go into shock. I discovered that Horatio is actually my father. My God, a few years ago, I might have produced a child with my half-brother had anything ever come of that relationship. I confronted Horatio with my "wonderful" news last night. He was as horrified of the implications as was I. He was understanding and willing to do anything to help me.

Ulrike stopped reading for a moment, reaching for a handkerchief to wipe away the flood of tears that invaded her eyes and totally blurred her vision. "Please excuse my reaction, your Honor. I can hardly believe what I am reading. Please do indulge me for a minute or so. I need to collect myself before I continue reading the remainder of my friend's letter."

"Ms. Hammer, please take all the time you need," responded Judge Horowitz, who himself had a difficult time hiding his tears. Rarely in his days on the bench had he been touched as he was at this moment by Juliana Knecht's confession. He was fully aware of Arabella and Sylvia's stifled sobbing in the back row of the courtroom. Realizing how he felt and listening to Ulrike Hammer's reading of the all-revealing letter from the grave so to speak, he wasn't about to act in this instance.

"Thank you, your Honor. I'm ready to continue." Ulrike picked up Juliana's letter and continued to read:

Earlier today we met again. Horatio handed me an envelope containing a note and the address of an abortion clinic in South Central LA. He included one thousand dollars. I would never have considered putting my life into the hands of such a man. I'm enclosing the money for you to use for more needed plastic surgery on your face. I searched for Horatio's note but don't seem to recall where I put it. I'm so befuddled, I don't know anymore what I will do next. All I know is that I cannot continue to live my life. Lord knows, what will happen at sea, but I'm prepared to meet my maker.

I'm fully aware of the impending storm but have every intention of sailing *Arabella* out to sea and ending my life. There's so much confusion at the yacht club in preparation for the impending disaster, no one will observe me sailing Horatio Jr.'s boat out of the harbor. I have secured a very sharp tool allowing me to quickly sever the mooring ropes, making it appear as if they were torn by rough seas and the horrendous winds expected.

Last but not least, I have taken a vial of cyanide from the dispensary and will resort to its use should things get too dicey during my odyssey at sea. But no matter which way it all shall end, I now say farewell to my earthly existence. I feel dreadfully sorry for you, my dear mother, and all who will be impacted by my desperate decision to end my life and that of our unborn child. I love you all with all my heart. May God forgive me.

Much love,
Juliana Arabella

P.S. I am mailing this letter to you from the Morro Bay post office before I begin my journey at sea after the sun sets and dusk settles over the harbor on this day, September 20, 1968.

As her blurry vision swept around the courtroom, she saw nothing but teary eyes and a sea of handkerchiefs and tissues. Ulrike herself was sobbing bitterly.

Hermione Grand rose from her chair and addressed the Court.

"Your Honor, I request that the letters presented by Ms. Hammer be placed into the records of this trial. There is no doubt as to the authenticity of the documents presented, and I move for dismissal, your Honor."

"So noted, Ms. Grand."

"Ladies and gentlemen of the Jury, you are dismissed. Thank you for your service."

Judge Horowitz used his gavel with deliberation. "Court is adjourned." As he rose to retreat to his chambers, Bailiff Butler had the last word.

"All rise!"

There were sighs of relief among those at the table for the defense. None had expected the turn of events and the outcome of the trial of Horatio Alvis III. Junior walked up to his father and gave him a big bear hug.

"Sorry, Dad, for all that you went through. Who knew? Just between the two of us, I loved Juliana too. I just didn't have the guts to do anything about it. Perhaps now that we know who she was, I might say my subconscious dictated my actions. We'll never know. I'm terribly saddened knowing how she ended her life." He turned away, not wanting his parents to see how he truly felt about Juliana's death.

The only person totally unaffected by what had just transpired was Veronica. She remained her cool and detached self. While she was inwardly pleased with the ultimate outcome of the trial, she would never have owned up to the fact. She was determined to hold onto Horatio Alvis III and his name—and make his life a living hell.

❉

Things were differently perceived in the back of the courtroom. Julien held Arabella firmly in his arms as she nearly collapsed during Ulrike's reading of Juliana's last words. Not in her wildest flights of fancy would she have envisioned the outcome of the trial. She had been one hundred percent convinced that Horatio III had murdered her daughter. It was only when her mind took her back to the earliest days of her relationship with Horatio that she recognized that she herself had been very much in love with and loved by the man who had unknowingly fallen in love with their own daughter.

"My God, I thought those kinds of things happened only in Greek mythology and tragedies and not among common mortals," burst Arabella.

"Julien, please take me away from this place. I see the sun is almost setting, and I must beg you to take me back to Cabrillo National Monument. I must set eyes on that vessel where Juliana chose to end her life. Please indulge me."

"Do you realize how dark it will be by the time we arrive at the beach? I don't even know if they barricade the access road before darkness sets in. But I will give it a try."

"Please do; I'm sure you have a good flashlight in the car. That should help us with getting down to the beach safely. And as always, I have my collapsible cane in my purse. I just have to touch that boat for a last time."

Homer and Sylvia Annapolis were likewise totally surprised by the outcome of the trial. Being in the big city had been an adventure for them. They planned to have dinner at one of the nicer and well-known restaurants in town. However, both she and Homer were so shook up by Ulrike's revelations that a celebration dinner seemed to be in bad taste. They decided it was best to retreat to their humble abode near the old Point Loma Lighthouse and digest the tragic events of the day.

"I agree, Sylvia. Let's do dinner in town at some other time. After this afternoon, I'm ready to just sit down at home with a good glass of wine and celebrate our many good years of contented togetherness. I do need to stop at the Lighthouse before we head to our place. I don't know if you noticed, I was wearing my sunglasses all day. Thank goodness, they are prescription glasses as well. But I do like my trifocals and a bit more light in my life. I must have left them on my desk last night. You won't mind if we make that quick stop, right?"

"Here I thought all day long you were wearing those dark glasses on purpose, trying to hide your eyes and your tears. I saw you crying a few times. You can't fool me after almost sixty-two years of living with you. That last witness really got to me, too. It must have been an absolute shock to Juliana's mother. No wonder she was so heavily veiled. Sorry to digress with my chatter.

"Of course, I have no objections for us to stop at the lighthouse. I wouldn't want to be without my regular glasses. Well, now that we have that all settled in our old minds, let's see if we can find our car in the underground garage. I know how much you love driving in and out of these places, and even worse, parking in those narrow slots. Let's go, my good man."

They walked out of the courtroom hand-in-hand.

Chapter 30

Sylvia hung onto Homer's arm. "I believe you parked the car on deck four; that's about as low as you can go. The parking space was #419, I distinctly recall."

"I'm glad you paid attention to that. My mind was in a total fog when we hurried toward the trial. I know it was my fault that we were late. I just hate driving in big cities, especially with all these one-way streets, broad boulevards, and round-abouts. I'll be a very happy man when we make it out of here."

"Just follow those arrows and the signs that say 'Exit' and you'll be just fine. I believe you must turn right after you pay the attendant for the parking. Don't be shocked, it will be a few dollars since we were here for most of the day. I'm thrilled it is all over and we don't have to make another trip into the city for a long time. I love being in our neck of the woods. Homer, watch out. You almost backed into that fancy car behind us. Couldn't you see that bright-yellow sports number? Are you sure you can drive with those sunglasses at night? Let's not get ourselves killed in the process of escaping the city."

"I'll see just fine once we are out of the garage. It's these bright florescent lights that really do a number on my corrected vision."

"You are OK now. Just follow those signs until you get to the pay booth. I'll watch out and let you know which way to turn to get out of this parking heaven."

Homer put the car in park and handed the parking ticket to the attendant.

"That will be eight dollars for the day, Sir." Homer swallowed hard but decided not to make any comments, not wanting to convey the impression he was a cheapskate. He handed the guy a ten-dollar bill. There was just the slightest hesitation before two bucks were handed back to him. He stepped just a bit too heavy on the gas pedal, making his tires squeal. "Would you believe it? I betcha that guy expected me to give him a twenty-five percent tip to boot. The nerve! Already I thought it was highway robbery."

"Relax, Homer. You need to turn right when you pull out of the garage. Then you travel for three blocks and make another right. That should be the road we'll take all the way to Point Loma. Now, wasn't that easy? All you need is a good navigator. You've been cooped up in lighthouses far too long. Now and then you should get out into this big, wide, and wonderful world."

"Sylvia, are you telling me that our life together has been boring?"

"No, not at all. But now and then it would be nice to be taken out for a nice dinner, see a play, attend an opera, go to a dance, and just plain live for the day. Is that so much to ask for? Do you ever listen to Loretta and Mary Henrietta when they tell us to do something fun and frivolous with the checks they send us for our birthdays and Christmas? Do you always have to be bound by that darn sea as Samuel is?

"The girls are right; we should now and then do something totally out of character for us. Life is indeed too short to always worry about saving. Saving for what? Joshua provided well for his wife. She inherited a lot of money from her parents when they passed. Mary Henrietta married well and is a successful businesswoman. And God forbid, if Samuel will ever get married, he'll be OK with his military retirement. We don't need to worry about leaving anything to the children. How often have we heard that?"

"I hear you," Homer remarked. "But think what we've been listening to all day. What wonderful lives did all these wealthy and educated people live? Besides that, I'm getting too old for some of these big-city adventures. I'll promise you, I'll take you out to dinner in our little town. There might even be a play at the school that we could attend. How does that sound?"

"You know I'll be happy with anything you want to try."

"Gosh, Sylvia, it is really dark once that sun goes down, especially on this road leading out to the lighthouse. I never thought I would miss the many streetlights in the city."

"What do you expect, driving with dark sunglasses at night? I told you it wouldn't be a snap. I'd lend you mine but your vision is so much worse. That could really throw you off your mark. Just drive slowly; there isn't another car in sight in either direction. You know most people in our neighborhood stay in after dark and don't like to drive at night. That will help you. You've got the road to yourself. It will be just a few minutes and you should see some lights on your right from the old lighthouse.

"I was thrilled to read in Samuel's last letter that he is planning to be home next Thanksgiving. He wants to be with all of us at the traditional feast and spend time with his mom and Mary Henrietta and her family. I can't believe those twin boys will be ten this year. Josh Jr. looks like his grandfather and you; Jason resembles more Jenna's line. Isn't it fascinating how the genetic pool seems to work? I'm so thankful that Joshua came into our lives when we were young and could give him all the love we had. He left us much too soon. Think about it, he was just about Samuel's age when he was killed." Tears were springing from her eyes as she reached over to touch Homer.

He didn't say very much and was seriously concentrating on his driving task, not wanting to veer off to the left where the drop-off was fairly steep. Homer leaned forward, wanting to improve his vision of the road.

"Do you see what I see?" he began questioning. "It's much too late for an afterglow from the sunset. Can you see the red in the sky in the faint distance? Do you see or smell smoke? I would step on the gas and get closer to the park in a hurry if I could see better. Can you detect anything with your regular glasses?"

"Now that you've called my attention to it, I can see more and more of a red glow as you are driving ever so slowly and closer to it. What do you think it could be? Could it be a brush fire after all the dry weather we've had ever since that storm in late November?"

"That's a distinct possibility," he observed. "Now, I can't wait to get to the lighthouse and my glasses. If it is a brush fire, I'll have to call the fire department. Thank God for the phone they recently installed in the visitor center. I have no doubt, we are looking at a major fire. It's a good thing we are not having a strong breeze coming off the Pacific. I'm on the pavement now and can drive a bit faster. Keep your eyes peeled on the left side; let me know as soon as you can make out what you can spot."

Just then they passed the last of the big trees lining the road; the opening afforded a clear view right down to the beach.

"Oh, no, no—my God, it's the stranded sailing craft that's fully engulfed in flames. It's just about all gone. Who would have done such a thing? Do you have your field glasses in the glove compartment?"

"Yes, I always have them with me. Let me pull over to the right. We need to get out of the car. Please, hand me my Zeiss lenses. I want to see if I can make out anything using just the binoculars. It's worth a try. It would save time not going for my glasses first." Homer raised the field glasses to his eyes.

Sylvia could tell from his facial expression that Homer might have seen a ghost. "Tell me, what are you looking at? Do you make out anything?"

"I'll be damned. Excuse my cussing. You won't believe what I'm seeing, Sylvia. There's a black car down there on that access road. I'm sure it's a Mercedes. Here's another shocker; close to the car stand two figures, their faces glowing brightly, reflecting the light from the roaring fire."

"Can you tell who they are?"

"My God, it's the lady shrouded in dark, Arabella, and her newfound love. He's got his arms around her."

"What are you going to do about it, Homer Elias Annapolis? Anything? Thank God it's no longer considered to be a crime scene. How could they get such a devastating fire started in such short order? It makes me wonder if they had planned to set the boat on fire."

"I have no answers to your questions. All I know is this: there's no danger to what's up this steep hill. The old lighthouse is well protected and isn't surrounded by flammable grasses, bushes, and trees. It's been done that way with purpose in mind. I won't touch this one or do anything about it."

"Are you telling me you're not calling the fire department or Commander Shepherd?" Sylvia's hands covered her face. It looked like she was trying to wish the fiery scene away.

"You understood me correctly; I won't tell a soul about it. We are looking at Juliana's immolation; it's the twilight of her life. Let the flames carry away the pain brought to the lady shrouded in darkness. What you and I are beholding at this moment shall remain our secret. We'll keep the Lighthouse mystery enshrined in our minds' eyes."

Sylvia couldn't help herself. She began to cry bitterly. "At least Arabella knows where Juliana found her final resting place. All we know is that Joshua is among eleven hundred and two souls drowned in the depth of the Pacific." Homer enfolded Sylvia in his arms.

"There, there, my love. Let's look upon this glowing fire as the triumphant closing chapter of the life of Juliana Arabella. Yes! And may the lovers viewing this final scene look to a brighter future. May they have as long a life together as you and I are still enjoying." He raised his field glasses as in a toast. "My good friend Avraham would proclaim: 'L'Chaim.' To life, indeed!"

Doretta's Damnation

Harald Lutz Bruckner

Chapter 1

HER screams were echoing down the marble stairway. Fernando charged out of his offices and rushed up the highly polished steps nearly taking a spill in his stockinged feet. He pushed open the doors to their private quarters in the palatial home of his ancestors, only to find his mother, *Señora* Esmeralda Garcia Lopez, and Doretta's personal maid, Donita, bent over Doretta who appeared to lie prostrate in their marital bed.

His mother fanned Doretta's face while Donita wiped away the perspiration on Doretta's brow and applied cold compresses. Doretta was mumbling outbursts in German although it was well known that her Spanish skills had markedly improved since her arrival in Santiago in April of 1963, now more than five years ago.

She seemed visually pleased when she glimpsed Fernando approaching her. "What happened? Did you have another nightmare?"

"I must have heard the marching of the guards outside. The sound took me back to events buried deep in my subconscious mind. You've been with me close to ten years and know how often the past invades my dreams."

Esmeralda Garcia Lopez touched her mantilla, pushing it slightly off her face. "When I walked into the room, she was yelling 'Momma, Momma, hold me, hold me!' I could tell she was having another nightmare and summoned Donita to assist with the care of your wife."

"Thank you, Mother."

Fernando touched Donita's arm. "Why don't you see my mother back to the breakfast table? I'm sure my father wonders what's happening. Please assure him that my wife is just fine and that she suffered with another bad dream. We'll be down in a while."

Donita held out her right arm to Señora Garcia Lopez who in a state of excitement had failed to carry her trusted cane. She had experienced a mild stroke two years earlier which left her with a slight limp on her left side but no further impairment. As soon as Donita closed the doors gently behind them, Fernando turned toward Doretta.

"Tell me what happened that frightened you so deeply? Was it the same dream? I'm always amazed how you can recall and speak of the events that torment you in your sleep."

"I found myself in that primitive bomb shelter in the arms of my mother. Moments earlier, three Nazis had dragged my father out of the house, practically beating him to death with their billy clubs and calling him a stinking Jew. There was blood everywhere. When I looked up at Mother, her dress was covered in blood spatters. I screamed for her to hold me as the sirens kept blaring and the sound of bombs striking near us frightened me to death. It was all so real. No matter how often those scenes play out in my nocturnal adventures, I never seem to be able to free myself of their impact on my existence. It's more than twenty-five years since I lived through those events."

"I try to understand, although I never lived through such traumatic events in my life. Perhaps, Dr. Rodríguez Amado was right when he advised you to write down some of these experiences in the hope that committing your thoughts to paper might ultimately free you of them. With your well-practiced typing skills, it shouldn't be too much of a challenge to do that. I will arrange for you to have total privacy in the office next to mine. Don't worry about style or writing a masterpiece; just put your thoughts down as you recall the events that plague you.

"It's a beautifully appointed room with lots of natural light and a pleasant view into our gardens were you to pause as you are looking up from typing. I'll bring in a designer and have the room changed to your liking, perhaps making it a bit less masculine.

"You know there is no need to worry about the children. As much as you love Federico and Alona, they will be well taken care of by servants. You can spend as much time with Federico when he is free of his tutor in the afternoons and you can always step away from what you are doing to peek in on Alona in her room. She won't mind stopping with whatever she is doing. What do you say?"

"Let me think about it. I need to take a shower and make myself presentable before I can join you and the others at breakfast."

She kissed Fernando lightly on his lips and let her vision follow him out of the room. Doretta freed herself of her negligee and stepped into the shower. She closed her eyes as she let the warmth of the water soothe her tormented body. When she opened her eyes to reach for the lavender soap, she could only scream in desperation. She was covered in blood from head to toe.

Fernando rushed in, seeing his wife shaking like an Aspen tree in late fall and dissolved in tears.

"Don't come near me and don't touch me. Turn off the blood and hand me that old blanket from the closet. I don't want to ruin your mother's precious towels."

"What are you talking about? What do you mean by turning off the blood? All I see is you in your wet nakedness." Fernando stepped into the shower, and in spite of Doretta's protestations enfolded her into his strong arms trying to soothe her wounded being.

"There, there. Just let me hold you. You are not covered in blood. Your imagination just ran wild with you. Please, don't let your nightmares invade your daily life. Come back to me; be the woman with whom I fell in love when we first met in Zürich ten years ago. I loved our walk-up apartment on the fifth floor of the old building. Walking all those steps up and down kept us in good shape, especially me, since I spent most of my days sitting in study halls exercising only my brain and doing little to stay vital. How I treasured making love to you in our cozy bed. You remember those days? How happy we were without all the trappings of my heritage."

"Thank you for holding me. You brought me back to reality. Don't frown on your heritage. Your family, other than your mother, has accepted me and has welcomed me and our children into your world of wealth and well being. It's a world I never knew of and never expected to surround me. I've learned to love your parents, especially your father. Your mother has a much harder time showing her love for me.

"Federico and Alona were the ones who opened her heart. Perhaps we should think about having another child; perhaps another boy, a second heir to the estate? Your mother often voices her concerns to me that something could happen to Federico. What would happen to the Garcia Lopez line? She regrets never to have been able to conceive another child after she gave birth to you. The way she often speaks to me, I wonder if she is attempting to place her guilt on me?"

"Let's not worry about mother. I want you to be happy. As to making another baby, I'm all yours. You want to give it a whirl?" Fernando freed himself of his shirt and trousers and nudged Doretta into the shower.